The Perfect

MATCH

The Perfect

MATCH

Janice Hanna

BARBOUR
PUBLISHING

Cover design: Faceout Studio, www.faceoutstudio.com

Published by Barbour Publishing, Inc., P.O. Box 719, Uhrichsville, Ohio 44683, www.barbourbooks.com

Our mission is to publish and distribute inspirational products offering exceptional value and biblical encouragement to the masses.

ecpa Member of the
Evangelical Christian
Publishers Association

Printed in the United States of America.

DEDICATION

To Julie Fletcher, Jana Meeks, and Danette Saye: I owe you so much more than a book dedication! Thank you for working so hard to make Courtney Elizabeth's bridal shower and wedding day so spectacular. I couldn't possibly have done it all without the three of you!

In this you greatly rejoice, though now for a little while you may have had to suffer grief in all kinds of trials. These have come so that your faith—of greater worth than gold, which perishes even though refined by fire—may be proved genuine and may result in praise, glory and honor when Jesus Christ is revealed.

1 PETER 1:6–7

CHAPTER ONE

HUNKA-HUNKA BURNIN' LOVE

I've always considered it wildly ironic that our local dating service—The Perfect Match—went up in flames. The incident happened on a Sunday morning, just as my husband and I prepared to leave for church. I caught a glimpse of something odd out the kitchen window, something that raised my sleuthing antennae. Stepping onto the back deck, I squinted, trying to make sense of the eerie red-orange glow that had appeared over our little town of Clarksborough, Pennsylvania. Within seconds, smoke rose in thick gray plumes, leaving a thousand questions running through my mind.

Our two miniature dachshunds—Sasha and Copper—began to run in circles, probably confused by the odd smell and the overwhelming sense of fear that suddenly gripped their owner. They've always had the uncanny knack of sensing my emotions, especially when I'm about to topple over the edge.

Convinced something was amiss, I turned back toward the house, hollering at the top of my lungs. "Warren, come quick! Something's on f–f–fire!"

My husband appeared at my side seconds later, his eyes

widening as he took in the scene off in the distance. Reaching into his pocket for his cell phone, he dialed 911. In an animated voice he shared what little he knew with the person on the other end of the line. Most of his words were choppy. . .frantic. Very uncharacteristic for my usually calm hubby.

Hanging up the phone, he turned my direction. "They said it's already been reported and firefighters are on their way."

As if to ditto his remarks, the piercing wail of a siren rang out. Though we couldn't see it—our house being four blocks from the center of town—I managed to focus my attention on the fire truck as it wailed its way by and did my best to figure out its destination.

As the noise faded into the background, I turned to Warren, barely able to breathe. "What do you think caught fire? The flower shop? The. . .the bank?" I spoke the words hesitantly, cringing at the very idea of his workplace going up in flames.

He shook his head as he responded. "No, listen to the siren. It sounds like it's farther south than that."

"Farther south?" Our son had only recently moved into an apartment in town to be near his workplace.

I reached down to pick up Sasha, who had taken to whimpering, and then mouthed a silent prayer, whispering a prayer for Devin's protection. He might be twenty-one, but he was still my baby.

"Don't worry, honey." Warren slipped an arm around my shoulder. "It's not that far south."

"But what else could it be?" I felt the sting of tears in my eyes and brushed them away. No point in borrowing trouble, as my very southern mama liked to say.

Warren strained to see beyond the row of houses across the street. "There's only one way to know for sure. If you're ready for church, let's go ahead and leave. Might as well see for ourselves."

"I'm ready." A quick glance down revealed that I'd forgotten to put on my shoes, but never mind that. I could slip them on in the car. I fetched them from my closet, checked my appearance in the hall mirror—groaning when I noticed the hair on one side of my head appeared to be cooperating more than the other—and made my way to the car, which Warren slipped into gear before I'd even fully closed my door.

As we pulled out of the driveway, I noted the time: eight fifty-five. My mind reeled with possibilities as we neared town, none of which brought me any sense of relief. Finally, we rounded the curve onto Main Street.

"Looks like the bank is safe," Warren said.

"And the flower shop. And the cell phone company." That meant. . .*Oh my goodness!*

"It's the dating service," he said.

Warren eased our SUV through the crowd of people now gathered on our little town's central thoroughfare. He deliberately avoided the area nearest the fire, sticking to the other side of the road. Still, we saw enough to make my stomach churn. As if it had waited until I'd arrived to show off, the shop's sign melted like butter on a slice of hot toast. Unfortunately, the rest of the building quickly followed suit.

At once my sleuthing antennae began to rise again. "Warren, who would do this? A jilted lover, maybe? Or someone unhappily matched?" I began to list all the many possibilities, and Warren finally turned to me, a warning look in his eyes.

"Oh no you don't, Annie. I'm sure this was just an electrical fire or something of that nature. It's an old building. I hear city officials have been after Opal for weeks to get this place up to code."

"Or. . ." I dove into a litany of other possibilities, my imagination working double time.

"Annie." Just one word, but it spoke volumes. My poor husband had watched me weasel my way into multiple investigations over the past few years and knew my penchant for making something out of nothing. Only this *wasn't* nothing. I could feel it in my bones. This was definitely something. . .and likely something I should investigate.

The beep of a cell phone interrupted my thoughts. My heart skipped a beat when I saw my son's number. "Devin?"

"Mom, I'm fine. Don't worry. It's the dating service. I can see the flames from my place."

"I know. We're within fifty yards of the building." I cringed as one of the windows shattered from the heat. Firemen worked diligently to douse the flames that shot out of it. "Honey, I have to go. See you at church."

"Okay, Mom." He paused and then threw in, "Don't get too close to the fire."

I sensed his real meaning, of course. He knew I'd be tempted to get involved, especially if I suspected foul play. And, of course, I suspected foul play. What super sleuth worth her weight in salt wouldn't?

We ended the call, and my heart grew heavy as I turned to Warren with the question neither of us had dared voice.

"Do you think Opal was inside?"

"Oh, I hope not."

I shivered at the very idea. Opal Lovelace—one of our town's quirkiest senior citizens—ran the facility. Had she survived nearly a century of major world shifts only to be taken down by the fiery flames of her forty-year-old dating service?

"Oh look!" Relief washed over me as I caught a glimpse of Opal, in her robe and slippers, talking to the police a couple of buildings down.

"Poor thing." Warren shook his head. "What's going to happen to her now? She doesn't have any family left in Clarksborough, does she?"

"Nope." *And now she has no place to live.*

Maybe Warren and I could do something about that. We had plenty of room in our home, now that our twin daughters were both married and Devin had moved to his own place. But what would my husband think of an eighty-three-year-old entrepreneur who'd outlived four husbands taking up residence in the spare bedroom? *Hmm. I'll ask him after service.*

A couple of minutes later we arrived at the church. Glancing out the car window, I caught a glimpse of my best friend, Sheila, standing near the front steps. She sprinted my way, her once red, now platinum blond hair setting her apart from every other parishioner. Well, that and the hot pink dress with large flowers draping the neckline. I leaped from my seat the minute Warren slipped the car into PARK.

"Oh, Annie! Did you see it?" Sheila grabbed my hand the moment my feet touched down on the parking lot. "The Perfect Match!"

I slung my purse over my shoulder and closed the car door. "I know. And what a bizarre coincidence."

"Coincidence?" She looked at me, her brow wrinkled in confusion.

"Just strikes me as odd—a business with the word *match* in its name going up in flames."

"Oooh!" Her perfectly painted eyebrows arched up, making the wrinkles around her eyes disappear for one magical moment. "Never thought of that. You don't suppose. . ." She gave me that same look I'd received half a dozen times before when we smelled a potential case brewing.

"I dunno, Sheila. Could be." I lowered my voice to a whisper as Warren approached. "But Warren wants me to stay out of it. He thinks I'm—"

"I think you're going to do whatever you feel in your gut is the right thing to do. No more and no less," he said as he passed by me. "And I wouldn't try to stop you for the world." He paused at the door of the church. "Just promise me you'll pray about this first, Annie."

"Of course!" I hollered out across the throng of people. "You know me! I don't do anything without praying first!"

About ten or twelve people turned to look at me, doubtful looks on their faces.

"Okay, maybe once or twice I got the cart ahead of the horse," I explained to my now-captive audience, "but I repented. And everything ended well." With a shrug, I turned back to Sheila.

"Opal's been facing financial woes for years," she said. "Ever since folks started using Internet dating services instead of places like hers. Can't help but wonder about that."

"Right." I leaned in to whisper the rest. "To be honest, I've never understood how she stayed in business at all, and not just because of her Internet competition. She's been through so much in her personal life. She's outlived several husbands, ya know."

Sheila nodded, her eyes widening. "Oh man. You don't think she had something to do with this, do you?" Lowering her voice, she added, "Like, maybe she wanted the insurance money or something because business was slow?"

"Maybe."

"The building needed a lot of repair. Maybe she torched the place, hoping insurance would pay to rebuild it. . .get it up to code."

"Who knows?" I shrugged. "I just know that something about this doesn't seem right. I have that niggling feeling I always get when I'm about to get pulled into something big."

"Me, too!" Sheila's eyes widened, her blue eye shadow disappearing into the tiny folds of skin.

The church bells clanged their customary Sunday morning welcome, and I startled back to attention. "Better get inside. I'll pray about this, Sheila. You do the same."

As I made my way into the sanctuary, my mind reeled at the possibilities. Yes, something was afoot with Opal Lovelace and The Perfect Match. The undeniable heat of a growing blaze lingered in the air. . .and I couldn't help but think the Lord had just handed me a hose.

CHAPTER TWO

HOT DIGGITY

I walked into the sanctuary of Clarksborough Community Church, astounded to see so few people seated. Glancing at my watch, I noted the time. Yep. Ten minutes after nine. Service should be starting in five minutes. Likely, most folks were distracted by the fire.

Not that I blamed them. We didn't get a lot of action in Clarksborough. Not really. Our little borough was a sleepy place, as a rule. Of course, there was that one time when our local florist was murdered. And then there was the incident with my son-in-law being kidnapped. And the bank heist a few months before that. But other than that, Clarksborough, Pennsylvania was the quintessential small town. . .quiet, peaceful, homey. Safe. And I wanted to keep it that way.

Settling into my customary pew—fourth row, left side, just off the middle aisle—I noted Warren's absence. Sheila, who took her usual place directly in front of me, turned back with a brusque nod. "We'll figure this out, Agatha Annie. I'm ready, willing, and able, so just let me know what you need me to do."

I nodded my response, not yet sure I wanted to figure anything out. Perhaps this time it would be best to leave things in the hands of our very capable police department.

From across the aisle, I caught a glimpse of my good friend, Louise McGillicuddy, and her fiancé, Nikolas Petracca. She mouthed, "I need to talk to you after service," and I nodded. Louise and Nick were getting married in a couple of weeks and had asked me to coordinate the event. These days I spent more than my fair share of time coordinating weddings. Not that I minded. Now that I'd married off my two daughters, I'd learned the ropes. . .and everyone in town seemed comfortable with Annie Peterson at the helm.

Our worship leader took his place at the front of the church and the music started. Drawing in a deep breath, I tried to relax. No point in staying keyed up through the service. But as we dove into the first worship song—a lively number that had my toes tapping and my hands clapping— my thoughts kept drifting to Opal Lovelace and her shop. Images of the charred building flashed through my mind, and I shivered. Who had done this? And why?

Warren joined me, slipping an arm around my shoulder and giving me a kiss on the cheek. . .his usual Sunday morning routine. But I could sense his nervousness today.

"Seen any of the kids?" I whispered, looking into his handsome face.

He nodded. "Devin just got here. He's sitting in back with a couple of the guys. Candy and Garrett are teaching kids' church this morning. She caught me long enough to ask if we were going out to lunch after church."

"What did you tell her?"

He smiled. "Told her yes, of course. They asked if we

could go to Petracca's." He quirked a brow and then winked at me.

"Whatever." I shrugged, wondering what everyone saw in Nick's new restaurant. Was I the only one in town who hadn't fallen in love with Greek food? I glanced once again at Louise, wondering how she felt about her fiancé's popular restaurant, with its traditional Greek fare.

I smiled at the look of bliss currently residing on her face and then looked around the familiar sanctuary for my oldest daughter, Brandi, and her husband Scott. *Hmm.* No sign of them. Maybe they weren't coming today. Maddy—their two-year-old—had been fighting the sniffles for days, after all.

About halfway into the song, I finally closed my eyes and did my best to focus on the Lord. This was certainly not the time to solve mysteries or think about Greek food. I had a firm belief that once one walked through the doors of a church, one should stay within the doors of the church— and that included one's mind and imagination. No rambling thoughts today.

As the music shifted into a familiar worship song, I gave myself over to doing what I'd come to do—worship. I did pretty well until we shifted to a new song that opened with the words, "Our God is a consuming fire." My thoughts, of course, diverted at once to the fiery demise of Opal's business. *Lord, help me stay focused.*

A tap on my shoulder caused my eyes to fly open. I couldn't help the grin as I laid eyes on Brandi. Behind her was Scott, who held a very feisty Maddy in his arms. The toddler was dressed in a darling purple and black ensemble, perfect for her fair skin tone. Her wheat-colored curls bobbed up and down as she fidgeted in her daddy's arms. I could hardly contain my joy; she was so precious!

Maddy took one look at me and hollered, "Nina!" her pet name for me. She did a swan dive in my direction, arms flailing.

"It's *Nana*, honey," I whispered, taking her into my arms. "*Nana*. Not Nina." Seemed no matter how many times we went over this, she still never quite got it.

Maddy giggled and whispered, "Nina."

I planted approximately twenty-five feathery kisses on both of her cherublike cheeks then scooted over in the pew, making room for the others.

"Sorry we're late," Brandi leaned in to whisper. "You-know-who threw her shoes in the toilet. Again."

Not this little doll! Not again! I hugged her a bit tighter, unwilling to believe such a thing.

"I didn't feel right putting her in the nursery, since she's not feeling great," Brandi added in a hoarse whisper. "Hope you don't mind if she sits with us."

"Mind?" I should say not! Of course, the bubbly two-year-old could be a handful, and she hadn't quite mastered the "Let's sit still and be quiet" thing, but this morning would give us plenty of opportunity to work on that.

I held her as worship continued. Maddy loves music and did well during that portion of the service. However, as Pastor Miller began to preach, she apparently found his sermon on Moses lacking. She began to squirm, so I tried handing her my keys to play with. That usually kept her preoccupied. After a few minutes of quiet play, she tossed them into the air.

Ack! They landed directly on Sheila's platinum blond head.

My best friend's overly dramatic "Ouch!" disrupted the sermon, if only for a moment. Pastor Miller looked her way with a half grin then continued with his message.

Sheila's husband, Orin, fished the keys out of Sheila's tightly sprayed locks and handed them back to me. I muttered a quick apology then tried to shift Maddy's attentions to my necklace. "Look, honey," I whispered. "Bling!"

The darling toddler spent a couple of minutes nearly choking me to death trying to get the necklace off. I finally gave in and removed it, placing it into her open palm. I'd lost more than one piece of jewelry this way, but she was worth it.

I'd just handed off the necklace when Pastor Miller said something that caught my attention. Something about God speaking to Moses out of the burning bush. Man! A fire theme? Was this simply a coincidence, or was the Lord trying to tell me something? Was He speaking to me out of the fiery embers of Opal's building? *Get involved, Annie! You can do it!*

Thinking about Opal made me wonder once again if she had a place to stay. My heart began to ache for her. No family. No close friends. And she wasn't the type to attend church. Never had been. Maybe. . .just maybe the Lord wanted to use me to reach out to her. *Stay focused, Annie. Stay focused.*

As Pastor Miller continued his message, I did my best to pay attention. There would be plenty of time to think about Opal later, to come up with a plan to help her.

At the end of the service, I made my way over to Louise and Nick. Louise grabbed my hand and looked at me with joy radiating from every pore. "Oh Annie! Can you believe our wedding is in thirteen days? Seems like just yesterday Opal was introducing us, and now we're about to be man and wife!"

"Well, you know what they say. 'Time flies when you're having fun'!" I laughed. "And I'd say you two have been having a blast getting everything ready for your big day." Their big fat Greek wedding was truly going to be the event of the season.

"Yes." Nikolas slipped an arm around Louise's shoulder, looked at her with love in his eyes, and gave her a gentle hug. "We can't thank you enough for your help with the wedding plans, Annie. There's no way we could've pulled this off without you. You're a lifesaver."

His thick Greek accent made me smile, as always. Something about the way he said my name tickled me.

"It's so exciting!" I said. "Have you decided where you're going on your honeymoon yet?"

"Oh yes!" Nick squared his shoulders, and his accent thickened as he explained. "After we get married, Louise will quit her job at the funeral home, and we will travel to Greece then on to Italy. I will make a world traveler out of her! We will be gone for six weeks. Then we come back to Pennsylvania to run the restaurant!"

I still couldn't quite believe it. Louise—the mousy fifty-something spinster who thought she'd never marry—had likely never left the *county*, let alone the country. And here she was. . .about to become a world traveler! With a handsome Greek husband, no less!

"You've got to come shopping with me, Annie," Louise

whispered in my ear. "I need some new clothes and um. . . other essentials. . .for my honeymoon."

"Ah ha."

I'd do one better than go shopping with her. Sheila and I would throw her a lingerie shower! And quick! I made a mental note to check for an available evening at the church. Surely the women's ministry could help with an impromptu shower for one of its own.

Warren approached. "Who will manage the restaurant while you're away?"

"Our usual workers will be there, of course. And my baby brother Elio will arrive from Greece this week. He knows better than anyone how to run a restaurant and will take over while we are away." Nick slapped Warren on the back. "You will love my brother! He is a laugh a minute! And you've never seen a better cook." Nick went off on a tangent about his brother's cooking abilities but lost me as he started talking about chickpeas and olives.

"He sounds great," I agreed. "But I sure hope he doesn't find our little town too boring."

"Boring?" Louise and Nick looked stunned.

"There's nothing boring about this place!" Louise said with a nod. "Especially lately!"

At that, our conversation turned back to the fire. Thinking of the fire made me think of Opal. Thinking of Opal reminded me that I needed to ask Warren if she could stay with us. And thinking about Opal staying in our home reminded me that I had some serious cleaning to do. We certainly weren't company ready.

Louise's voice provided just the right distraction. "We're

headed to Petracca's for lunch. From what I hear, half the church is going! Would you join us?"

Her words, like a magnet, drew my children to our side.

"I can't wait!" Candy said, licking her lips. "It's been four days since we've been to Petracca's, and I feel like I'm going through withdrawal!"

Garrett added a quick, "You guys have the best bread in town."

"And have you tried their salad?" Sheila asked, joining our ever-growing circle. "Oh, I could eat it all day! That feta cheese is the best. And they've got the best olives in the world." She began to list the many varieties of Greek olives, nearly losing me altogether.

I offered up a forced smile. Yep. Looked like I was the only one in Clarksborough who hadn't boarded the "Let's eat Greek!" train.

Oh well. If I couldn't beat 'em, I might as well join 'em. With flames of doubt licking my heels, I headed off to Petracca's for an adventurous lunch with the people I loved.

CHAPTER ⚏ THREE

KEEP THE HOME FIRES BURNING

Warren and I had just reached the bottom step at the front of the church when Sheila caught me by the arm. "Did you see that?" she asked in a hoarse whisper, as she gestured to the crowd on our right.

"What?" I tried to follow her gaze to see if I could figure out who—or what—she was talking about.

"Don't look!" Anxiety tinged her voice, making me more curious than ever.

"How will I know who you're talking about if I don't look?" I asked, my arms now crossed. My gaze darted to the right, more to tease her than anything.

"Annie, don't," she whispered. "If you'll be still, I'll tell you." She lowered her voice a bit more and leaned forward. "It's Chris Brewster and his wife."

"Chris and Kathy? What about them?" I tried once again to turn to get a look at Clarksborough's most famous dueling pistols—er, happily married couple—but she stopped me.

"They're arguing. Again."

"Ah." A gentle shrug was about all I could muster. No big news flash after all. Chris and Kathy were usually arguing. At times I had to wonder why they'd married in the first place.

22

I'd never met a more unlikely pair. Still, Opal boasted to everyone in town that she'd played a role in bringing Chris, our local newspaper editor in chief, and Kathy, a wannabe actress from New York, together. In fact, she'd written about them in her "Happily Ever After" column in the *Clark County Gazette* just a few weeks back.

"I don't know why they feel so free to carry on in front of the whole church like that," Sheila added. "Seems like they'd keep it behind closed doors." After a moment's pause, she added, "You can look now. They've turned the other way."

I pivoted on my heel, taking note of my "number one son-in-law," as Scott liked to call himself, headed over to chat with Chris. *Hmm. Wonder what that's about.* Seconds later, Brandi joined them. I saw her expression shift from one of joy to concern as they talked.

"What do you make of that?" Sheila held up a church bulletin so Chris and Kathy couldn't see her.

"I have no idea. But Scott's a great conversationalist, so if anyone can get information out of them, he can."

A couple of minutes later, Brandi approached with a somber look on her face. She shook her head and mumbled, "That's just so sad!"

"What, honey?"

"Oh, Chris Brewster just told Scott something that broke my heart. Opal Lovelace is staying in that awful little motel on the turnpike tonight because she's got no place else to go."

"No way." I'd driven by the Stumble Inn hundreds of times, cringing more as the years rolled by. The old motel should've been torn down ages ago. Why in the world would

Opal have gone there, of all places? Was she hurting for money? Couldn't afford a nicer spot to rest her weary head? My heart ached more than ever. We had to remedy this. . . and quick!

Scott joined us, holding a now-sleepy Maddy in his arms. He picked up on our conversation and offered a few more details. "Opal's got no family and very little money saved, so the police are talking about putting her in a shelter in Philly for a few weeks. Least that's what Chris said. And he usually gets the scoop on just about everything around here."

"A shelter?" My heart leapt into my throat. *Not while I'm living and breathing! I can't picture Opal living in a place like that!* A chill shimmied its way up my spine at the very thought of it.

"That's why Chris and Kathy were arguing," Scott added. "Kathy had this harebrained idea that Opal should come and stay with them. Chris disagreed, of course." Scott laughed. "Can you even imagine adding Opal to that mix? It would be like pouring gasoline on an already-blazing fire!"

"Well, Kathy probably feels compelled to offer, since Opal is the one who introduced them."

"What about Opal?" Warren asked, approaching from behind us. "Something else happen?"

"She's got no place to go!" I looked at him with imploring eyes. "How sad would it be to be eighty-three and have no one to care for you? And they're talking about putting her in a shelter in Philly. A *shelter*."

"Hmm." He seemed to be pondering the situation.

Again I looked at him, offering my most woeful expression. "C'mon, honey. What do you think? Would it be okay? Could Opal come and stay with us?"

He looked stunned. "What? Like, at our house?"

"Well of course!"

"Are you serious?" Scott's eyes grew wide.

"Oh Mom, I think it's a great idea," Brandi said, offering my first glimmer of hope. "The perfect solution." God bless that oldest daughter of mine! She understood.

"What's perfect?" Candy and Garrett asked in unison as they joined us.

"Mom and Dad are taking in Opal Lovelace!" Brandi exclaimed for all to hear. Several people turned our way with stunned expressions on their faces.

"For how long? You mean, a night or two? Or. . ." My darling hubby's voice trailed off.

"I don't know." I drew in a deep breath, thinking about our options. "As long as she needs. We've got plenty of room, now that all the kids. . ." A lump rose in my throat the size of an orange.

Warren pulled me close and placed a kiss on the end of my nose. "Feeling that empty nest thing again, huh?"

"Maybe." I swallowed the lump and looked at him with my most hopeful expression.

"And you're thinking an eighty-three-year-old woman with an obnoxious cat is the perfect substitute for a houseful of teenagers?" Scott asked with a dubious look.

"Oh my goodness! She has a cat!" I cringed as the realization hit. How could I have forgotten Opal's ten-year-old tabby, Don Quixote? "Maybe she could leave the cat with a family member or something."

Brandi laughed. "Mom, if Opal has no family to stay with

herself, what makes you think she's going to have a place for her cat?"

Warren shook his head and offered a winsome smile. "No, it's okay. She can come and bring her cat. But we'll have to keep a close eye on Sasha and Copper. They're liable to have Don Quixote for lunch."

"Are you kidding? Have you *met* that feisty feline?" I got sidetracked informing him about the kitty's wild and woolly ways then finally came back around to the matter at hand. "So, it's okay? We're going to offer Opal Devin's room?"

"I guess." He sighed. "But I can't imagine she'll really be comfortable in there. She's going to go from lace curtains and doilies to football pennants hanging on the wall and the lingering odor of dirty tennis shoes seeping from the closet."

"Hey, I got rid of that smell a couple years ago," I reminded him. "And if I know Opal, she'll make herself at home." And who wouldn't, in our house? We Petersons had a real knack for making folks feel welcome, or so I'd been told. Must be my southern upbringing and the instilling of my mama's "Hostess with the mostest" mentality.

"I'm trying to imagine what it's going to be like to live with someone that age." Warren shook his head. "We'd better stock up on Geritol and fiber pills."

Okay, he had me there. "Very funny. I'll have you know Opal's in better shape than either of us. She walks three miles a day."

"Hmm. Probably trying to get away from that cat," Scott suggested.

"No, she takes the cat with her. She walks him on a leash," Brandi said. "I've seen her."

"Walks a cat on a leash?" Warren closed his eyes, as if trying to picture it. "What have I said yes to?" He slapped himself in the head, and we all laughed. Everyone within hearing distance knew Warren had a heart of gold. He could no more turn away Opal Lovelace than I could stop editing manuscripts. Or solving crimes. Or planning weddings. Or meddling in my grown children's lives.

We agreed to take up the conversation once we reached the restaurant. Since Petracca's was just a few blocks from the church and had limited parking, we all decided to walk together. What a crowd we made—the whole Peterson clan, along with Sheila and Orin. As I looked around the group, a feeling of joy washed over me.

Thank You, Lord, that my daughters and their husbands live nearby. I know not every mother of grown children has that. May I never take it for granted.

Minutes later, we approached the colorful Petracca's, Clarksborough's newest eatery. I braced myself for the inevitable. Would I find anything. . .*normal*. . .on the menu? Sure, the others were bound to eat with abandon, but likely I'd go home afterward and make a grilled cheese sandwich.

As we entered the restaurant, I noticed Teresa Klein, one of the women from the church, seated alone at a table. I offered a smile at the fortysomething then headed her way.

"Hey Teresa."

"Hi Annie." She brushed a loose hair from her face. "Looks like we all had the same idea."

"My family is more into Greek cuisine than I am," I explained. After a moment's pause, I added, "I don't know if you can stand the chaos at our table, but you're welcome to join us. We'd love it, in fact."

"Really?" She looked up at me with hopeful eyes. "You wouldn't mind?"

"Mind? Of course not! Please do."

"Thank you." She reached for her purse and tagged along on my heels as I headed toward our family table.

"Isn't it just awful, what happened to Opal's place?" I asked, making small talk.

"I guess." She took the seat to my right and shrugged. "But if you ask me, Opal needed to shut that place down years ago. She's got no business telling people she'll find them a match made in heaven when all the men she pairs you up with end up being. . ." Teresa looked at me and sighed. "Sorry. I promised myself I wouldn't go there. Just because she hasn't been able to match me up with someone doesn't mean I don't wish her well."

"Ah." I'd forgotten about that. In fact, I hadn't spent much time thinking about Teresa Klein's dating life or lack thereof. We weren't really close. I had my family, and she had. . .

Hmm. To be quite honest, I didn't know what she had, other than her job at the grocery store and a handful of friends. I occasionally saw her at church, of course. And our paths crossed at a variety of holiday festivities in the park. But we didn't travel in the same circles. Perhaps today the Lord was nudging our circles together.

Our server—a young kid named Greg—took our drink orders and returned shortly after, trying to balance the tray without losing it. He managed to get all our beverages delivered without a single mishap.

From across the table, I heard Orin mumble, "I'm starving."

"You're always starving," Sheila chided him.

After that he muttered something about how he'd missed out on the usual donuts in Sunday school this morning. I laughed. "Men and their stomachs."

"Hey, we always have donuts," he said. "But for some reason they were MIA today."

"You poor thing." I offered my best sympathetic look. "I'm not sure how you made it."

"Must've been torture." Sheila gave him a wink.

"No kidding." Orin sighed. "A man's gotta have his donuts."

I'd just taken a sip of my diet soda when Louise and Nick came through the front door of the restaurant.

"Look at that," Warren observed with a nod. "The place has only been open twenty minutes and Nick is already here. He can't be away for a minute." My husband chuckled. "He told me he wasn't working today, that he'd leave it to his employees. Go figure."

"Makes me wonder how he's going to get along on that lengthy honeymoon." I smiled, understanding such a strong work ethic. I shared it. In fact, between my editing work and my recent jaunt into grandmotherhood, I barely had time left over to sleep. Or cook. Or clean house.

Hmm. I wonder if Opal is the domestic sort. . . .

Just then, Louise showed up at our table. "You look like a happy bunch. We must be doing something right. Everyone got their drinks? And you've ordered?"

"We have." I offered a smile. "Why don't you join us,

Louise? Sit awhile and rest. You're not on the clock. Just because you're marrying into the restaurant biz doesn't mean you have to wait on us, honey! Take it easy."

"Oh, I don't mind. In fact, I love it here." Her eyes sparkled as she explained. "For thirty years I've worked at the funeral home, where I sit all day long. Most all day, anyway. And I've always seen people at their lowest. Here. . ." She gestured around the restaurant. "People smile. They laugh. They're enjoying their family members. Not. . ."

"Burying them?" I threw in.

"Right." Her eyes brimmed over as she leaned down to whisper. "I've returned to the land of the living, Annie. And I love it. So don't worry about me being on my feet. I'm having the time of my life, and I'm thrilled that Nick needs my help. Trust me."

Oh, I trusted her all right. In fact, she had me so worked up, I felt bad for having said a word. "In that case," I said, "we'd like some more of that. . ." I pointed to the empty plate in the middle of the table. "What do you call that stuff again?"

"Hummus?"

"Yes. That mashed chickpea stuff. It's not half bad." In fact, the flatbread was downright wonderful. Maybe I'd have to give this Mediterranean food another shot.

"Nick has the best recipes in town. They're his grand-mother's, you know." Louise started talking about Nick's Athenian grandmother, which got me to thinking about Opal. Thinking about Opal reminded me that we needed to swing by the motel on our way back home to offer her a place to stay. Thinking of Opal in my home immediately filled that empty space I'd been struggling with since Devin moved out.

Oh what fun I'd have, with Clarksborough's busiest matchmaker under our roof. And how wonderful that she'd be right there as she searched for the perfect match for Devin. Yes, this was surely an idea from on high.

As Louise headed off to fetch more hummus, I glanced down the table at my only son. His more-than-troubled love life had always concerned me. Slightly on the tubby side, he wasn't the sort most girls would find hunky. And he'd dropped out of college after only two years, in order to pursue his dream of web design. That wasn't exactly winning him brownie points with the opposite sex either.

Oh, but if only the girls could see beyond the fluff to peer into his heart. Then. . .then they would find the giant teddy bear I knew and loved, the one who never forgot a birthday, who always cared enough to call whenever he needed counsel, and who loved God with his whole heart. If they could watch him lead worship in the youth group or hear him pray. . .then they would know the man of God I knew.

Devin had signed up with Opal's service at my gentle nudging, but so far she hadn't found the right girl for him. If I brought Opal into my home, surely she could focus on Devin, locate his perfect match.

Yes, this was just the ticket. If anyone could fan the flame of hope for my son's ailing love life, Opal Lovelace could.

CHAPTER FOUR

RING OF FIRE

On Monday morning, after we finally convinced Opal she should join the Peterson clan until her situation improved, she packed up Don Quixote in his worn-out crate and tagged along behind me in her beat-up Chevy to her new home. . .the Villa de la Peterson. My excitement mounted as we drew near the house. I could see the relief in Opal's eyes and was pretty sure I even heard her sniffle.

I ushered the petite, white-haired darling into the house, thrilled when I thought about the possibilities ahead. Sasha and Copper met us at the door, yapping like maniacs. Sasha did a high-flying acrobatic act in an attempt to reach the crate that held the rambunctious feline. Opal, to her credit, held it tight, in spite of Don Quixote's high-pierced shrieks of displeasure from inside. Sounded like he might very well scratch his way out with little trouble. Then what would we do?

"Oh my goodness!" Opal looked stunned. "My poor little kitty!"

"Well, we're off to a good start." I ushered the dogs into the laundry room and told them to stay put and behave until further notice. "Sorry about that," I said, as I headed back to the foyer. "They'll adapt in time. Now, let me show you around your new home."

Opal's eyes widened as I walked her into the spacious living room. "Oh Annie! It's beautiful. I haven't been in your house since your kids were little and we had that Women's League luncheon here." She elaborated about how much time had passed, and I felt guiltier by the moment.

"I haven't been very neighborly, have I? Sorry about that." A frown quickly rooted itself on my face. For the second time in two days, I felt guilty about not being a better friend to those around me. Was the Lord burning a new message in my heart, perhaps? If so, Annie Peterson was on the case! *I'm listening, Lord, and I will respond!*

"I tell you what I'll do to repay you for your kindness." Opal reached for my hand and gave it a gentle squeeze. "I'm going to work extra hard to find a wife for your sweet boy, Kevin."

Kevin? Did she mean Devin? "You really mean that?" I managed. "Oh, I hope you find her! I've been hoping and praying the right girl would come along, but for some reason she's eluded us." *Oh Lord, I know Your timing is perfect! Please bring the right mate for my son.*

A ripple of laughter escaped from my petite guest, and she patted my hand. "Kevin's perfect match is out there, and I'm going to find her." With a wink, Opal added, "Oh, and don't worry, honey. I won't charge you a penny for my services. You and Darren have been so kind to invite me into your home."

"It's Warren."

"Right, right. Warren. Nice fellow. Great salt-and-pepper hair. Decent build for a man in his early fifties. Handsome face. And a wonderful, steady job at the bank. That's a plus." After a moment's pause, she added, "I would've paired you up with someone a bit different, though."

"O–oh?" That certainly got my attention.

She turned to me once again. "You're such a peach, Annie. Filled with vim and vinegar. Darren is a nice boy. He's just a little. . ."

What?

"Boring." She patted my hand again. "But never mind that. I'll turn him into the man of your dreams while I'm here."

Lovely.

Opal yawned. "Just show me to my room. Don Q and I need a little nap." She clutched the crate that held the temperamental tabby.

We arrived at the room that, for years, had housed my only son. Opal's nose wrinkled at once. "Oh my." She sneezed. "Well, it's a lovely room. Lovely." A second sneeze erupted. "Though I do detect a bit of a. . .what would you call that. . .odor?"

"Odor?" I shrugged. "You smell something?"

"Well, I hate to voice any complaints when I've only just arrived, but it does smell a bit like old shoes in here, doesn't it." She patted my hand again. "But don't fret, honey. I'll just open a window. Hope the heat from outside doesn't give me a headache. Sometimes I get headaches when it's too warm. But never you mind that. I'll be fine."

My goodness. Now what?

She reached to take Don Quixote out of his crate. "Is it safe, dear?" She looked around, perhaps thinking the dogs might join us in a free-for-all with her beloved kitty.

"They're behind closed doors," I assured her.

She pulled the somewhat frantic tabby cat from his crate.

"Oh, what a little. . ." I started to say "sweetheart" as I reached to scratch him behind the ears, but he hissed at me, his eyes glowing an eerie orange. I withdrew my hand in a hurry. *No thank you.*

"Never you mind him, honey," Opal said. "He'll warm up to you in no time."

I sure hope so.

With the cat firmly shoved under her arm, Opal approached the window and attempted to open it.

"Oh, here. Let me do that." I pushed it up and adjusted the curtains to allow a breeze to enter the room. Seconds later, the heat from outside wafted in, along with a hint of a breeze.

"Oh, much better. I can barely smell the foot odor now." She nodded then looked around the room. "Though it's liable to warm up in here mighty quick." After a pause, she leveled a piercing gaze on me. "Do you mind if I ask you a question, Annie?"

"Of course not."

"Well, this is lovely décor and all." She pointed to one of Devin's football pennants. "But hardly suitable for a long-term stay."

"L—long term?" I swallowed hard, thankful Warren wasn't hearing this.

"Would you mind if I found some lace curtains for the

windows? And I think a lovely mirror would be nice above the dresser, don't you? That way I can see to put on my makeup before going out."

Sheila and I had often noted that Opal wore an exaggerated amount of makeup for someone her age. For someone of *any* age, for that matter.

"Well, I suppose—" I started.

"Yes, a mirror is in order," my new guest interrupted, looking around. "I spend at least an hour every morning putting on my face." She turned to me with a wink. "You know what I always say, honey. 'A man's face is his autobiography. A woman's face is her work of fiction.' "

Okay, I had to laugh at that one.

"I like to keep the illusion going," Opal added, "but that takes serious work, great products"—she pulled out a makeup bag from her suitcase—"and a great mirror." Opal gestured to the wall space where the pennants now hung.

"Oh, of course." I nodded, ready to make my guest feel at home. "Anything you like."

Opal rambled on and on about several of her clients as she unpacked her bag. Clearly, the woman was proud of her matchmaking skills. Still, I had to wonder. . .if she was so good at pairing up folks, why hadn't she found someone for herself?

"Did you see the article I wrote about our newspaper editor and his lovely bride?" Opal asked with a delighted look on her face. "It just came out awhile back."

Yep, I'd seen it. To say she'd taken some liberties in her description of Chris and Kathy as a happy couple would be a vast understatement. She'd made them sound like the most harmonious folks in town, when nothing could be further from the truth. Still, I wouldn't debate the issue with her.

"I can't figure out why Chris has been so testy the last few times I've talked to him," she said with a sigh. "It's so out of character."

"Well, we all go through ups and downs," I said. "I'm sure he and Kathy will mend their fences."

Her eyes narrowed to slits, and she began to fan herself with her hand. "Goodness, gracious! Don't tell me there's something going on with those two. Why, they're my prize customers! My best advertisement." Opal started talking to herself about how news of this nature could destroy her business. Never mind the fact that her place of business had burned to the ground.

"I'm sure everything is fine between them," I reassured her.

"Of course they are. They're a match made in heaven. Yes, I wish every couple came away as happy." She muttered something under her breath, and I thought I heard her mention Teresa Klein's name.

"What about Teresa?" I asked.

"I never thought I'd say this about any of my clients. Truly." Opal's brow knotted, and she twisted her hands to-gether. "But I do believe that woman is an impossible case. Truly impossible."

"Impossible?" My curiosity rose at once. "Why would you say that?"

"I sent her several perfectly good matches, and she turned down every one. Talk about picky. This one was too fat. That one was too thin. This one was too tall. This one was too short." Opal shook her head. "I daresay, she's been a thorn in my side for months now. And can you believe she asked for her money back? Honestly!"

Well, this was quite a revelation. A clue, perhaps? "Did you give it to her?" I asked. "The money, I mean."

"Heavens, no. I have—or rather, *had*—a mortgage to pay." Opal's already-pale face turned one shade lighter as she pondered what she'd just said. "Hmm, that brings up an interesting point. Does one have to go on paying one's mortgage if one's home burns to the ground?"

"Good question. Better contact your mortgage company to make sure. But I'm assuming you were insured, right? Won't they take it from here?"

"Thank goodness I'm well insured. I updated my policy just two weeks before the fire. Lucky for me!"

Interesting coincidence. I made a mental note, suddenly reminded of Sheila's words: *You don't think she had something to do with this, do you? Maybe she wanted the insurance money or something because business was slow.*

A couple of seconds later and the idea latched on good and tight. Had Opal burned down her home—her place of business—for the insurance money? Did I have a pyromaniac living in my house?

Suddenly I had an overwhelming desire to hide the matches.

CHAPTER FIVE

OLD FLAME BURNING

I'd heard the saying "Silence is golden, but duct tape is silver" all my life but never really pondered its meaning. By the end of the first night with Opal in our home, I understood it completely. Opal was like a record that never stopped playing. . .one nitpicky critique after another. Our house was too hot. My cooking left something to be desired. Sasha's bark was annoying. Copper needed to lose weight. I needed more exercise. The refrigerator smelled like mustard. Our deck needed to be swept. On and on the list went, nearly driving me beyond the point of thinking clearly.

Less than an hour into the second day, I thought I'd snap like a twig. Sasha had spent that hour growling at Don Quixote from across the living room. Copper—who always liked to give second, third, and fourth chances, even to the most undeserving—tried on several occasions to sniff at the feline in an attempt to make friends. But Don Q, as Opal liked to call him, wasn't playing nice. I'd never heard so much hissing and squalling. Opal commented nonstop about all of the above, repeating things over and over until I seriously thought I might have to leave the house.

What have I done? Lord, save me!

By that afternoon, I'd made up my mind to work harder at making things better. I planned a delicious dinner with the whole family, deciding to cook chicken fajitas, my girls' favorite. To my great delight, Opal offered to bake a cake. She headed off to the kitchen to locate the necessary ingredients while I—grateful for the distraction—wrote out a grocery list.

I happily made the run to the grocery store, taking more time than necessary to shop. I even paused at Teresa's register and chatted about the weather and the upcoming ladies' retreat at the church. Finally, after stalling as long as I could, I headed home.

Arriving at the house, I found the electricity out. No problem. We had a gas stove. I could still move forward with the meal plans. Surely the lights would be back on by the time the kids arrived. If not, we'd move the party outside to the deck. That way Maddy and the pups could play in the yard while the grown-ups visited.

Making my way into the kitchen, arms loaded with grocery bags, I found myself distracted with meal plans. However, a noise coming from the area in front of the stove stopped me in my tracks. I squinted to make sure I was seeing correctly. Opal's head was in the oven, her amply padded rear and stocking-clad legs sticking out behind her.

"Oh honey, no!" I dropped the bags onto the counter and knelt beside the poor thing, my heart aching. "I know you're distressed about losing your home, but this isn't the answer." A lump rose in my throat as I pondered the things that must've led her to such a drastic move. And to think I'd been so short-tempered with her just a couple of hours ago!

Had I somehow driven her to end it all? Was I really that difficult to live with? *Oh Lord, forgive me! What have I done?*

Opal pulled her head out of the oven and gave me a curious look. "What isn't the answer?"

"Well. . ." I pointed to the oven. "This."

"If you want me to bake a cake, this *is* the answer," she insisted. "Now back out of the way. I've got to get this pilot light lit. Crazy thing went out when we lost power, and I haven't been able to get it going again."

"Oooh!" I rose to my feet, relief sweeping over me. Thank goodness! Only then did I notice the box of matches in Opal's hands. Seeing them reminded me of her building—flames leaping from the windows. "Here, Opal. Let me do that."

She stared up at me and groaned. "Okay. Can't get the confounded thing lit, anyway. I was never very good with matches." She handed me the box, and I helped her to her feet—no small task. Her joints appeared to be locked tight.

As I lit the pilot, she emptied my grocery bags. . .a friendly gesture. "Oh, chicken. I love chicken." She held up the package of chicken breasts with a smile. "Seems like ages since I had a good, home-cooked meal. Yummy."

"I'm making homemade chicken fajitas," I bragged. "The girls claim mine are the best they've ever tasted. I'm from the South, you know. We eat fajitas all the time in the South. But no one in Clarksborough cooks them like I do. Oh, and just wait till you taste my salsa. I hate to brag, but it's mighty good. . .especially if you like a little spice."

"Fajitas? Salsa? Oh, I see."

"What's wrong?" I asked as I rose to my feet. "Don't you like them?"

She patted my hand. "Well, I can't eat spicy food, honey. That's all. Rough on the intestines, you know. Is there anything else you can make for me?" She gave me a pout, and I struggled with the feelings that washed over me.

Patience, Lord. That's all I'm asking for.

Perhaps taking her cues from my delayed response, Opal said, "Well, never you mind about that, Annie. I'll just make a peanut butter and jelly sandwich to nibble on while the rest of you are eating real food. Don't you worry about little ol' me. I'll be just fine." She walked out, muttering, "Of course, I'm supposed to be watching my sugars, so peanut butter and jelly might just send me into a diabetic coma, but that's okay. I'll manage somehow."

Lord, give me patience. Lord, give me patience.

I put the cake into the oven, forging ahead with the meal preparation, finally deciding I could bake one of the chicken breasts for Opal. Plain. No spice. Surely that would make her happy. I'd just popped it into the oven at five fifteen when Warren arrived home.

"How was your day?" he asked, wrapping me in his arms.

"Mm-hmm." I didn't dare say more. How could I admit defeat after just two days? No, I'd better keep up the illusion, at least for a couple more days.

"I see." He stepped back and stared into my eyes. "If you need me to get you out of this, Annie, just say the word. I have it on good authority Pastor Miller and Evelyn have offered to take her if this doesn't work out."

"Really?" Man. The temptation was overwhelming. Still, I hated to oust my guest after such a short stay. Didn't want to scar her for life. She'd already been through so much, after all. Besides, I hated to give up when the task had only just begun.

"Ask me again tomorrow," I whispered. "I'm still in watch-and-see mode."

"Well, if she stays, we're all liable to end up in the paper. You know how desperate Chris is for a story. He's already covered the fire down to its last detail. He'll probably want to do a follow-up on Opal, now that she's staying with us."

"Oh? What do you mean?"

Warren handed me the *Clark County Gazette*. "Headline story. Read it for yourself."

I scanned the LOCAL BUSINESS GOES UP IN FLAMES headline. Chris hadn't missed a detail about the fire. It was all there, along with photos of the devastation. I cringed as I stared at Opal's former home. Looked like she wasn't going back anytime soon. No, more likely the city would tear the place down and she'd have to rebuild.

Turning back to my meal prep, I did my best to stay focused. After all, tonight's dinner would be the perfect distraction. I glanced in the oven at Opal's piece of chicken. So far, so good. Just a few minutes more. I'd put a smile on her face after all. . .if it was the last thing I did.

Candy and Garrett were the first to arrive. "I've been on my feet all day at the salon," Candy groaned as she entered the living room. "Do you mind if I sit? I'm exhausted all the time lately. All I want to do is drop into bed as soon as I get home in the evenings."

"Hope you're not coming down with something."

"And if you are, I do hope you're not contagious, dear." Opal took a step backward as Candy settled onto the sofa nearest her. "My immune system isn't what it used to be, I'm afraid."

"Oh, I'm fine." With a wave of a hand, Candy declared herself fit as a fiddle.

Brandi and Scott came through the door minutes later, with Maddy in tow. I still marveled at how different my twin girls were. While Candy—the younger of the two—was a little more hesitant in her approach to life, Brandi was Type A all the way. And apparently it had seeped into Maddy, who raced my direction, arms extended.

"Nina!"

"That's *Nana*, honey. *Nana*."

The toddler rubbed at her runny nose with the back of her hand and smiled. "Nina!"

"Sorry. Maddy still has the sniffles," Brandi explained as she reached to wipe her daughter's nose with a tissue. "I don't know what's up with her. It's been going on for weeks."

"Oh dear, oh dear." Opal strategically took a seat on the far side of the room and began to fan herself. "Has she had her shots?"

"Shots?" Brandi turned to Opal with a stunned look on her face. "Do you mean her immunizations?"

"Well, I don't know what they call them, dear," Opal said, growing pale. "But I know puppies and children get shots for a variety of diseases so that people like me don't catch them. If she hasn't had her shots, would you mind keeping her at a distance, please?"

Brandi snatched Maddy into her arms and followed me to the kitchen. "Well, I guess that answers my question about how it's going."

"Um, right." I lowered my voice to match hers. "I don't know how long I can keep this up, to be honest. She's pretty high maintenance."

"I can see that."

Scott entered the kitchen and mouthed the word, "Wow." We all nodded in response.

I'd just started to open my mouth to share my angst when I heard Opal's voice. Turning, I saw her shuffling into the kitchen.

"What's burning?" she asked.

"Oh." Yikes. "I'm baking you a piece of chicken. I think it's almost done." I opened the oven door and peeked inside. "Yes. Caught it just in time. A minute more and it would have been—"

"Burnt." She stared at the chicken, pursing her lips. "It's burnt. Well, I suppose I can eat it anyway. I'll peel off the skin. Of course, that is my favorite part, but I don't guess I need the calories anyway. Of course, a plain burnt chicken breast isn't much of a meal, but I suppose I'll manage. At my age, one doesn't need many calories anyway, I guess. Just enough to get by. Of course, with all of these sick people around me, I could use the sustenance, but never mind that."

Lord, give me patience. Lord, give me patience.

I drew in a deep breath and counted to ten as I pulled the baking dish from the oven. I hadn't managed to edit for a single client today, thanks to my houseguest. And now I couldn't even enjoy dinner with my family.

Despite the lights coming on, I still opted to serve dinner on the back porch. "It will be like a picnic," I explained.

We'd no sooner stepped outside than Opal declared she

would catch her death of cold, what with the chill in the air. *In June?* She headed off to her room to grab a sweater before she joined us at the picnic table.

After we'd prayed for the food, Devin finally made an appearance. "Sorry, Mom. I was playing video games with the guys. We got caught up in it, and I lost track of time."

He took his seat and reached for the tortillas. He pulled one out and loaded it with chicken, onions, cheese, sour cream, and salsa. All the while, Opal stared at him as if he'd grown a third arm.

"What?" Devin asked between bites.

"Well I hope you won't take this the wrong way," Opal said, "but I'm never going to catch you a bride if you go on eating like that."

"Eating like what?" He shoved another bite into his mouth and gave her a curious look.

I glanced her way with warning in my eyes. How dare she critique my baby boy and his eating habits? So he was a little tubby. Who cared? The right woman would see beyond all of that.

To her credit, Opal didn't respond. Instead, she continued to stare at my son in rapt awe as he shoveled bite after bite into his mouth.

Candy—my compassionate one—turned to Opal, perhaps in an attempt to distract her from Devin's eating habits. "I'm so sorry to hear about what happened to your place," she said. "It's shocking."

"Yes, tragic," Opal agreed, turning to face her. "Thank goodness I'm well insured; otherwise I don't know what I'd do." She took a little nibble of her chicken then made a face.

Placing the fork back down, she put her hands in her lap.

"Will you reopen your business once the new building goes up?" Devin asked, his mouth again filled with food.

"Well of course! I've still got a lot of good years left in me. I'll just take a little sabbatical between now and then. But I can't stay away for long." She turned to Devin and winked. "There are still plenty of folks needing my services. And a little instruction on how to win over someone of the opposite sex."

He choked on a piece of chicken then swallowed a large gulp of water. Likely the idea of Opal Lovelace attempting to get involved in his love life—or lack thereof—still scared him to death. After the events of the past couple of days, I couldn't blame him. What had ever made me think she might be capable of doing. . .well, anything. Anything productive anyway.

No, after watching her in action, I couldn't imagine her arranging a meal. . .let alone a marriage.

CHAPTER ⧘⧘⧘ SIX

FIRE AND RAIN

After three days of catering to Opal's every whim, I was nearly ready to throw in the towel. Just about the time I'd worked up the courage to telephone Pastor Miller to deliver my concession speech, Opal decided Don Quixote needed a trip to the vet's office. One sneeze from the feline was all it had taken to convince Opal he was allergic to Sasha and Copper. Allergic my eye. That cat was too mean to be allergic to anything but himself.

With Opal away, I had the opportunity to collect my thoughts. Perhaps I hadn't given this enough time. Yes, I could surely hang on another day or two.

That decision made, I was able to arrange a quick meeting with my bride and groom. After all, we were down to ten days, and there were a zillion loose ends to tie up. I telephoned Louise at Petracca's, hoping she and Nick had some free time. With the boisterous crowd in the background, I could barely make out her words.

"Nick has gone to the airport to pick up his brother," Louise hollered. "They should be back from Philly in a couple hours."

"Ah."

"Why don't you meet us at the restaurant at four, Annie. We need to finalize the reception menu with Janetta."

"Right, right." I smiled as she mentioned Clarksborough's caterer extraordinaire. "I'll give her a call. If the time works for her, I'll be there."

We ended the call, and I rubbed my ear, wondering if my hearing would ever be the same. "Man, that place does *some* business."

Though Janetta sounded plenty busy when I called, she assured me she had the afternoon free. I heard something odd going on in the background but couldn't quite put my finger on it. Was someone praying. . .over a loudspeaker? *Where is she?* Unfortunately, she hung up before I could ask. Oh well. There would be plenty of time later, once we met.

To kill some time while Opal was at the vet's office, I cleaned the toilets. Then scrubbed the bathroom floors. Then rearranged the pantry. Then cleaned the oven. Finally convinced I'd handled all the issues Opal had brought up over the past few days, I plopped down on the sofa, exhausted. I needed to pray about the situation, needed to do some serious intercession, but dozed off instead. Surely the Lord understood my exhaustion. Right?

Opal arrived home minutes later with a groggy Don Quixote in her arms.

I shook off my sleepiness and attempted a concerned look. "What's the verdict?" I asked, noticing how doped up he appeared.

"Anxiety disorder," she said. Pursing her lips, she stared at Sasha. "Caused by the dogs."

Naturally.

Opal promptly declared she and Don Quixote needed a nap. I would have curled up for one myself, but a glance at my watch told me I had just enough time to freshen up my hair and makeup and get to Petracca's for my meeting.

I entered the restaurant at four as planned, the over-powering scent of Mediterranean food accosting my senses right away. Glancing around, I took note of the fact that the crowd had thinned. Not that folks would stay gone long. Likely the dinner guests would arrive within the hour.

Louise and Nick greeted me right away. A handsome fellow with dark curls and a thick moustache stood beside Nick. Except for the difference in age—this man being a good ten or fifteen years younger—they could've been twins.

"Annie, I'm happy to introduce you to my brother, Elio." Nick beamed as the handsome stranger extended his hand my way.

I shook it and nodded. "Nice to meet you. How was your flight?"

"Oh, what a time I had!" The handsome stranger went on to tell me several stories of people he'd met between Athens and Philadelphia. I smiled—as much from his thick accent as his exaggerated stories. I liked Elio right away and knew others in our tiny community would get a kick out of his beautiful accent and boisterous laugh. And surely every single woman in town would find him attractive. No doubt about that.

Janetta entered the restaurant minutes later. She looked breathless and a little scattered, returning to her car to fetch her notebook. A consummate pro, she rarely let others see her in such a state.

"Goodness, girl. What happened to you?" Louise asked as Janetta finally took a seat at our table.

"Oh." Her cheeks flushed. "I, um, had a delivery."

"Food?" I asked, looking up from my notebook.

"Well, a care package. I've been doing that prison ministry thing with Richard."

"Oooh, right." I nodded. One of our parishoners—Richard Blevins—had just been released from prison last year and had started a ministry to the men he'd met while there. Still, there was something about the look on Janetta's face when she mentioned Richard's name that made me suspicious. In a good way.

"I had no idea you were involved in Richard's ministry, Janetta." I gave her a warm smile. "I'm so glad to hear it."

"He's doing so well, Annie," she said. "He has such a heart for those men. Can you believe what the Lord has done? Seems like just yesterday. . ." She paused and shrugged, not finishing the sentence.

I remembered the incident well. Richard, a former bank employee, had stolen cash from a night deposit, hoping to cover the cost of cancer treatments for his wife, Judy. Sadly, she'd never lived to have those treatments, and Richard paid a high price for his crime of passion. Interesting, though, that Janetta had linked arms with him. Who would have thought it?

Louise offered her a sympathetic look. "Such a wonderful ministry. I'd want someone to visit me if I was ever in prison."

"Like you've ever done a bad deed in your life!" I laughed at the very idea.

The lines between her brows deepened. "Yes, but Annie. . . it wasn't so long ago—less than three years, in fact—that you thought I murdered Fiona."

"Oh, well there was that." I had accused her of murdering our town's beloved florist, Fiona Kelly. But I was wrong and didn't mind admitting it—then or now.

"Somehow I doubt we'd be such good friends if I'd actually committed murder," she said.

"Well, I would come see you in prison, no matter what you'd done." Janetta reached to take her hand. "If I've learned anything from this prison ministry, it's that we're all sinners in need of God's grace."

"Amen to that," Louise said with a nod.

"Yes indeed," I added. In that moment the Lord whispered, *"And Opal needs an extra dose"* to my heart.

"I'd be the last person on earth to judge someone else," Janetta said with a sigh. "I've only known the Lord a few years, and I can't help but remember what the old Janetta was like. If you don't believe me, ask my kids. Kristina and Jakey will tell you. So who am I to point out the speck in someone else's eye. . .ya know?"

Yeah. I knew, all right. A part of me wanted to point out the specks in Opal Lovelace's eye, but I'd managed to resist, at least so far. Didn't want to spoil my testimony, as my mama would say.

"Hey, speaking of people doing time, has anyone figured out who burned down Opal's business?" Nick asked.

Elio's eyes widened. "Sounds like I missed something pretty big."

"You sure did," Louise said. "And to be honest, I'm dying

to know who did it, too."

"Wait." I looked at her, stunned. "Do we know for sure now that the building was deliberately set on fire? Is the jury in on that? I mean, how do we know it wasn't an accident. . . an electrical fire or something like that?"

"Oh. . ." She grinned. "One of our lunch customers heard it from one of the deputies. He said they were pretty sure the fire had been set. They even found traces of gasoline on the back side of the building."

"Oh wow." So my instincts had been right all along. Someone had torched The Perfect Match. Someone with a vendetta, likely. I was glad Opal wasn't around to hear all of this. "Arson. Hmm. Good to know."

I'd no sooner voiced the word aloud than images of Opal with her head in my oven came to mind. *Just a coincidence, surely. So she likes to play with matches. So what?*

"Let's get busy planning your wedding!" Janetta said, offering the perfect distraction. "I'm going to have to really budget my time, now that I've decided to try out for that television show."

"Television show?" I turned to her, stunned.

"Yes, you know the one. The Food and Family Channel does this competition called Super Chef."

"I've heard of it, of course," I said. "But I had no idea you were thinking of trying out!"

"Yes." She blushed. "Richard has really been encouraging me to. If I win the big prize, I'll get my own TV show."

"Good gravy!"

We all got a laugh out of that.

"Let's get cracking," Janetta said, looking at her watch. "Time's flying."

We spent the next hour going over every detail, from the layout of the very traditional ceremony to the foods and entertainment for the over-the-top Greek reception.

"I've never done a Greek wedding before," Janetta said, "so I'm relieved you're providing some of the food and offering recipes for the rest. I want to get this right."

"Of course, of course!" Nick clasped his hands together. "Another reason why I'm glad Elio is here. He's the best chef in the world. Wait till you taste his lamb and onions. And his baklava is all the rage in Athens." Nick went off on a tangent about their family's restaurant back home in Greece, but my attentions remained on the details of the wedding. There would be plenty of time to talk about all of that later.

"Really?" Janetta gave Elio an admiring look as he passed by. "Elio's the best chef in the world?"

"Yes," Nick said. "Or my name isn't Nikolas Petracca!"

"You just take care of the appetizers and the wedding cake, Janetta," Louise said. "And Elio will cover most of the rest."

"I'm good with that!" Janetta grinned and then gave handsome Elio another look.

Yep. The single women were certainly going to find him difficult to resist.

"Let's talk through the reception plans one more time," I suggested. "Did you speak to Pastor Miller about the Greek dancing? Is he okay with that taking place in the fellowship hall?"

"He said he would make an exception to the rules for us," Louise said with a smile. "And it's going to be so much fun. . . for all our guests. Wait till you see, Annie. Greek receptions are so lively. Lots of family-style dancing."

"I can't wait."

Just then, the bell above the door jangled as Teresa Klein entered. I flashed a smile, and she took a few cautious steps in my direction, clutching her purse in her arms, her gaze darting back and forth. Poor thing. I'd never met anyone quite as shy. Must be tough to have to travel all by her lonesome to restaurants.

As she reached our little group, her gaze shifted to Elio, and a hint of a smile graced her face. "Hi, Annie." She spoke to me, but her sparkling green eyes gave her away. They were firmly planted on Elio Petracca, and there they remained, though I tried valiantly to draw her attention my way as I spoke.

"Hi, Teresa." I gave a little wave, but might as well have been talking to a brick wall. She gave me a "Mm-hmm," but couldn't seem to unlock eyes with our newest citizen.

"Lovely lady, let me introduce myself." Elio stood and extended his hand. I could see the hesitancy in Teresa's expression. She turned her head, as if trying to figure out who he was talking to. Finally, she slipped her hand his way. When he kissed the back of it, she looked as if she might faint. For that matter, Louise and Janetta looked as if they might faint, as well. No doubt. None of us had ever seen Teresa look at a man with such intensity before. He was strikingly handsome, so I couldn't really blame her. In fact, if you looked closely, he might remind you of a hero from Greek mythology. I could see how a woman might be drawn to those chiseled features and his stately posture.

Clearly, Elio liked what he saw in Teresa, too, though I

must admit it took me a moment to figure out why. I'd never really thought of her as pretty—though she did have a nice figure and a pleasant smile. Today's upswept hairdo did show off lovely high cheekbones. And those eyes! I'd never seen them twinkle like that before. No wonder he was drawn to her. The woman was practically swooning at his feet.

"I am Elio Petracca, Nick's brother," he said. "His *much younger* brother, naturally. From Athens."

"N—nice to meet you." Teresa's cheeks deepened in color and her gaze shifted to the ground.

He pulled out a chair and gestured for her to take a seat.

"Oh, I don't want to interrupt," she said, looking more flushed than ever. "I—really, I just came to grab a bite to eat."

"What do you like?" Elio said, rubbing his hands together. "I make you a feast. You name it, I make it!"

"Oh, I just wanted a sandwich," she said, looking flustered. "One of those gyros."

He gave her a brusque nod. "Then I will make the best gyro you have ever eaten, or my name isn't Elio Petracca."

He turned back toward the kitchen, and she whispered, "Gyro. Elio Petracca." Her eyes looked as if they might tumble out of their sockets at any moment. Louise, Nick, Janetta, and I turned in silence to face her. After a moment, she seemed to come to her senses. "Well I. . .um. . .I guess I should probably get my own table so you can get back to wedding planning."

"Oh no you don't," Louise said, grabbing her hand. "Not so quick. You're staying put."

"I am?"

"You are." Louise chuckled. "I'm not going to miss this

for the world." Dear, sweet Louise. No doubt she understood Teresa's feelings better than anyone at the table.

Of course, Janetta was single, too. *Hmm.* Was I the only married person in the restaurant? Wow. Maybe our resident matchmaker needed to get back to work ASAP.

As my thoughts shifted to Opal, I realized she must be awake by now, doing heaven knew what to my house. I'd better get home to make sure Sasha and Copper were in one piece. Glancing at my watch, I noticed the time. Five thirty? Yikes! Forget the dogs. . . . I needed to get home to make sure *Warren* was in one piece!

CHAPTER ⛫ SEVEN

BURN, BABY, BURN

Sheila and I had a standing date at the local gym on Thursday mornings at nine. Determined to make it without any confrontations with my houseguest, I slipped out of the house while Opal was out taking her walk. As I turned the key in the ignition, a rush came over me. I'd never been so happy for a clean getaway.

I'd spent several minutes praying and reading my Bible this morning, determined to improve my relationship with Opal. There had been some comfort in the "tried by fire" scriptures I'd found. According to what I read, I would come out of this refined. . .if I could just stand the heat. Not that I particularly enjoyed the heat, but the refining part sounded promising.

I'd leave the refining of my soul to the Lord, but I had a feeling He wanted me to work on my body myself. So, off to the gym I went. I didn't mind leaving Opal alone, really. By now she knew her way around my kitchen well enough to fix a bowl of cereal. And I. . .well, I had a few calories to burn. Despite my former high-carb, low-exercise lifestyle, I'd finally come to grips with reality. These thighs weren't going away unless I actually did something about them.

With that in mind, I made the drive to the gym. Minutes later, dressed in respectable workout attire, I stepped onto the elliptical machine, ready for my routine. A few seconds into the workout, I already felt a difference in my legs. They turned to Jell-O beneath me. I ignored the feeling and chanted, "Burn, baby, burn," my usual way of coping with the pain of a good workout.

Glancing at the door, I saw Sheila entering. She'd pulled back her Clairol-blond hair with an eighties-style headband in a flaming hot pink. As if to further advertise her age, she wore a tie-dyed leotard, with black leggings poking out beneath. My poor friend must've gotten lost in an exercise-induced time warp. She'd donned a Jane Fonda/*Flashdance* getup that only a menopausal woman could appreciate. Maybe *hot flash dance* would be more appropriate.

She drew near and pointed to her outfit. "What do you think, Annie? I found this in a box in the attic. Had it for years."

"Mm-hmm." *What to say. . .what to say. . . ?*

"Makes me feel young."

My mind reeled backward in time. I couldn't escape the Richard Simmons *Sweatin' to the Oldies* images that flashed through my memory as I stared at her. I increased my pace on the elliptical machine, feeling the heat. *Burn, baby, burn.* "That's really something, Sheila." My stock answer in a jam.

"Have I mentioned how much I hate to exercise?" she groaned as she dropped her gym bag and climbed onto the elliptical machine next to mine. "To my way of thinking, exercise is a dirty word. Every time I hear it, I wash my mouth out with chocolate."

I had a good laugh at that one but did my best to focus. *Burn, baby, burn. Burn, baby, burn.* The pain in my calves reached an unbearable point, but I refused to give up. I'd promised myself this summer would be different. I'd given up the nightly ice cream ritual and focused on exercising. I swallowed enough water every day to fill a river. And I'd located the bathroom in every shop in town.

Sheila leaned my way with a knowing look in her eye. "I've got news."

"Oh?" I looked at her with some degree of curiosity— the sort brought on by something other than her outfit. "What's up?"

"I'm not sure," she whispered, "but I think there must be something going on at the sheriff's office." Her eyebrows elevated mischievously, as they always did when she had news to share.

"Oh?" I tried not to act overly interested but secretly longed for information.

"Yep. Orin says they've just hired a new deputy."

"Really?" I almost lost my pacing at that announcement. "Has someone left?" Hopefully not O'Henry. I'd leaned on him for several cases thus far. To lose my favorite deputy now would be devastating, particularly with a new mystery in front of me.

"No, no one's leaving. Orin says with the crime rate on the rise in Clark County, they just need more officers. But this time. . ." She looked around to make sure no one was listening then lowered her voice. "Well, let's just say this one's different."

"Different?" I pondered the possibilities. "Different color?

Different age? Different language? What?"

"Different. . .sex. She's a girl!" Here Sheila clamped her hand over her mouth and began to laugh. "It's about time, don't you think? In the cookies of life, women are the chocolate chips. And we've had way too many bland cookies over the years in this county, if you catch my meaning."

I caught it, loud and clear. Still, I could hardly believe it. Clark County had always been a little behind the times. They hadn't started using computers in patrol cars until two years ago and had only just updated their facility. To think, they'd finally hired a female deputy! It *was* about time!

I huffed and puffed on the elliptical, now feeling the burn both in my legs and my arms as I moved back and forth, back and forth. "What do you know about her?"

"According to Orin, she's a baby," Sheila said. "She's in her early twenties, has flaming red hair, freckles, is really petite, and. . .oh!" Sheila stopped midsentence, her gaze shifting to a young woman crossing the gym floor with a towel in her hand.

I stared at her—the girl, not Sheila—doing my best not to slow my pace. I'd never seen this particular woman at the gym before, and she matched the description Sheila had just given perfectly: early twenties, red hair, freckles, petite. Innocent-looking, even. Certainly not the sort I'd take for a rough-and-tumble cop. "Do you think that's her?" I mouthed.

Sheila nodded and mouthed, "Has to be."

We focused on working out, but I kept a watchful eye on the young woman, the one the trainer called Molly. While I didn't note anything overly suspicious, it did strike me as odd that she was one tough mama on the workout equipment. Her rough-and-tumble-cop side was starting to show, after all. In fact, she put us to shame with her vigorous approach to bodybuilding.

Sheila and I had just wrapped up our workout when my cell phone rang. I answered with a breathless, "Hello?"

"Mom?"

I could hear the emotion in Brandi's voice.

"What happened?" I asked, reaching for my keys. It would only take five minutes to drive to Brandi's house from here, and from the sound of things, she needed me.

"It's Spike." Her voice quivered with emotion.

"Spike?" I put the keys back down and breathed a sigh of relief as I thought about their fluffy little canine. "What happened to him?"

Brandi erupted in tears. "Nothing. He's fine. It's just that Maddy's pediatrician said. . ." More tears. "He said Maddy's *allergic* to him."

"Oh no!"

"Yes. And Mom, he told us we have to remove Spike from our home for a week or so to see if Maddy's sniffles stop. After that, we might have to make a permanent decision."

Uh-oh. Tell me it ain't so. . .

"I don't really have anyone else to ask. Devin's in an apartment, and Candy can't do it because she and Garrett are both gone all day. So I was wondering if you and dad would. . ." Her voice trailed away and a shiver went up my spine. Did I really have room in my world—my home—my backyard—for her hyper Maltese mix?

Of course I did. How hard could it be, really? If I could handle an eighty-three-year-old woman and her anxiety-driven cat, how tough could a little Maltese-dachshund be?

CHAPTER EIGHT

ONE LITTLE SPARK

Taking on the extra dog proved a bit more problematic than I'd figured. Turned out, Spike had one of those I'm-going-to-bark-until-the-cat-is-out-of-the-house mentalities. After several hours of yapping—and man, can a dach-tese yap—we were all about ready to leave the animals in the house and move to a hotel. Or another country. We hadn't really decided yet. Add to that the pain in my legs from overdoing it on the elliptical machine, and I was in rare form.

I finally managed to get things under control after dinner, putting Spike, Sasha, and Copper in the master bedroom while Opal and Don Quixote headed off to her tiny room. That done, I decided a bubble bath was in order. If anyone deserved a long soak in the tub, I did. Besides, it was the only privacy I'd had all day.

While resting in the warm bubbly water, I thought back over the events of the past few days. I'd acquired three houseguests—an eighty-three-year-old matchmaker, a ten-year-old tabby cat, and a feisty Maltese mix. So much for Empty Nest Syndrome. I'd give just about anything to have a quiet house once again but could tell that wasn't going to happen anytime soon. No, it was much more likely Opal would stay on through eternity, and the animals and I would grow old together.

And poor Warren! He'd been as good as gold about all this, but I could see the exhaustion in his eyes. He'd spent all day working at the bank, only to arrive home to a zoolike environment. By nine o'clock, the man was already in bed, watching the news on television. I joined him after my bath, whispering a thousand "I'm sorrys" for the way things had turned out. In his usual good-natured way, Warren kissed the tip of my nose and told me I was the godliest woman he'd ever met. Oh, if only he could see the awful thoughts rolling around in my head about Opal. Then he would know I was anything but! Again, my thoughts shifted to my "refined by fire" Bible reading. Hopefully I could hang on a bit longer without things heating up. *Lord, is there any way to refine me without involving fire?*

By ten fifteen, I found my eyelids growing heavy. Before long, I dozed off, and a crazy dream kicked in. In my dream, we were all at Opal's house, in the midst of the fire. The dogs were yapping to beat the band, chasing Don Quixote through the flames. Opal raced about, searching for her glasses and her laptop. Warren stood with a hose in his hand, showering us all with a powerful spray of water. And I. . .well, I stood there in shock and silence, frozen stiff. Unable to move. Off in the distance, Opal began to scream at the top of her lungs.

Tossing and turning, I finally awoke. Turned out, Opal's high-pitched screams weren't just in my dream. I could hear her from Devin's room, a terrified sound in her voice as she called my name. "Annie! Annie, come quick!"

"W–warren?" I nudged him, and he sprang up right away.

"What happened?"

He didn't have to ask twice. Opal's blood-curdling wails sent him sprawling out of bed. I joined him, reaching for my robe. Sasha, who'd been sleeping under the covers, shot out in a high-pitched fit of barking. Copper—ever our protector—yawned and rolled over, snoozing again almost immediately.

As I stepped onto the floor, I realized my legs didn't want to function properly. In fact, they ached something fierce and felt wobbly. So much for my time on the elliptical machine. I hobbled a few steps and then paused. Hobbled then paused. *Oh, the pain!* About halfway down the hallway I smelled something. . .odd. What was that?

Seconds later, the high-pitched sound of the smoke detector answered my question.

"Fire!" Opal came barreling from her room with Don Quixote in her arms.

Warren, being the only levelheaded one in the group, instructed us to wait in the hallway while he dashed into her room. "It's a candle on the bedside table," he called out. "Must've tipped over."

He ran to the kitchen to grab the fire extinguisher and quickly returned to douse the flames, which now lapped the wall and the edge of the comforter. I pushed open the window and turned on the ceiling fan, hoping that would quiet the smoke detector. By now, the smell of smoke permeated the hallway, and Opal began to cough. Before long, the cough turned into choking fits.

"I think you should wait outside," Warren called out. "Go on, Annie. I'll come and get you when it's safe to come back inside." He pulled the comforter from the bed and moved

Opal's laptop to the far side of the room.

We headed down the hallway, through the living room, and out onto the back deck, where Opal stood trembling, her beloved kitty cat in her arms. Sasha whimpered nonstop and scratched at the back door, trying to get back in the house.

"Stay calm, Sasha," I pleaded, reaching down to rub the backs of my calves. "Daddy needs time to fix this without you under his feet."

A few seconds later, the alarm shut off. "Thank goodness. Looks like he's got it under control." The trembling in my hands finally slowed. I hesitantly opened the door and entered the kitchen, still trembling from the shock of it all. "How did this happen?" I asked Opal as we made our way across the dark room. "Any idea?"

"No. I. . .I don't know." Her answer sounded truthful, but I could hear the fear in her voice.

I reached to turn on the light and gasped after I turned back to my houseguest. Whoa. I'd never seen Opal without her face on before. The woman who stood before me looked tiny, shriveled, and pale. I'd never noticed how pronounced her wrinkles were. And her hair! Much thinner than I'd realized.

Opal's hand immediately went to her head, and she gasped. "Oh Annie. . .I didn't want anyone to see me like this." She giggled. "I guess my little secret is out."

"Secret?"

"I wear spare hair," she whispered.

"Spare hair?"

When I shook my head, she said, "You know. . .a wig.

During the day I wear a wig."

And a mighty lot of makeup. I hardly recognized the barefaced woman standing across from me now.

Warren finally entered the kitchen, a look of exasperation on his face. Well, exasperation mixed with relief. "I got it. Wasn't too bad, really. No serious damage. But another few minutes and. . ." He shook his head. "Well, the whole place could've gone up in flames."

"Oh my, oh my. . ." Opal's eyes filled with tears.

Warren looked Opal's direction, his jaw dropping as he took in her appearance. To his credit, he kept his thoughts inside his head. God bless that husband of mine. "Tell me everything that happened. . .in order," he said, taking a seat at the table. "Don't leave out a thing."

Opal proceeded to tell him that she'd drifted off to sleep reading a book, with the prettiest red pillar candle lit on the bedside table. "I. . .I guess I bumped it?" she offered. "In my sleep, I mean."

"Well, it's a good thing you woke up when you did. Not sure why that smoke detector took so long to go off. Really puzzles me." He pursed his lips, and I could see the concern in his eyes.

After a few minutes of talking, I suddenly remembered something. "Oh my goodness!"

"What, Annie?" Warren gave me a curious look.

"Copper is still in our bedroom. I hope he's okay."

"He is. I checked on him. Sleeping like a baby."

"And what about Spike. Where. . .where is he?"

"Oh, I don't know," Warren raked his fingers through his hair. "Never thought to look for him. I'm pretty sure he's in his dog bed in our room. That's where he was when I was watching the news earlier. Do you think he could've slept through this much racket?"

"Surely not."

I searched the house with Sasha on my heels. Copper came when called, but not Spike. Checking the master bedroom, I found him missing. Oh no! Had he somehow gotten out when we slipped out the back door?

"Oh Warren, Brandi's going to kill me. I've lost her dog."

We walked to Opal's room and paused in the doorway, hearing a strange thumping sound from underneath the bed. *Whack, whack, whack, whack.* On and on it went. . .a sound I knew quite well. A dog's tail hitting the leg of the bed.

I tiptoed to the edge of the bed and dropped to my knees. Sure enough, Spike had taken up residence under Opal's bed. "Come here, you mangy mutt." I took hold of his collar and gave a tug. It didn't take much effort to snag the little mongrel. Holding him in my arms, I scrambled to my feet then sat on the edge of the bed.

"He must've gotten in here while I was sleeping and knocked over the candle." Opal nodded, a look of exasperation replacing her former penitent look. "That explains it. These dogs are a menace. A real menace, I tell you."

Though I hated to blame the dog, I had to admit, it sounded like a viable answer. "You almost burned the house down, you goofy thing." I scratched Spike behind the ear. I turned my attentions to Opal. "Was your door open, hon?"

"I got up to go to the bathroom," Opal said, clasping a hand over her mouth. "Maybe I didn't close it all the way? I don't know."

"Well, I guess that answers our question." I gave Spike a nuzzle. "We have a naughty dog on our hands."

"*All* dogs are naughty," Opal mumbled.

Instead of responding, I decided to get to work. We spent the next half hour changing the sheets on her bed and scrubbing soot from the wall. The candle had left a few burn marks on the table, but they were minimal. And Warren had already handled the cleanup of the wax, thank goodness.

Exhausted, I finally headed back to my room. Warren and I climbed into bed, three dogs now nestled between us under the sheets.

"Will you ever forgive me?" I asked.

"For what?" He yawned.

"You know." I sighed. "For taking in an eighty-three–year-old woman and our daughter's dog."

"And a cat."

"Right. The cat."

"Honey. . ." He turned to face me, bumping into Sasha, who let out a growl from beneath the covers, "I love you. You can bring as many people. . .and canines. . .into this house as you please, and I'll go on loving you."

"But if I hadn't said yes to Brandi about Spike, we wouldn't have had a fire. For that matter, if I hadn't invited Opal, there wouldn't have been a fire. So, in essence, the fire is my fault."

"It wasn't much of a fire," Warren said, stifling another yawn. "So go to sleep. All's well that ends well."

"I guess."

He rolled over, and I lay on my back, staring into the darkness. Something about tonight's events troubled me, but I couldn't put my finger on it. I played and replayed the incident over in my mind, trying to grab hold of the thing that worried me.

Finally it hit me. I sat straight up in the bed and gasped. The dogs took this as some sort of alarm and jolted from underneath the sheets, growling as if we were under attack.

Warren groaned and turned my way. "What is it, Annie?"

"Warren. How did Spike get into Opal's room?"

"You heard her. She left her door open. Case solved. Go to sleep." He rolled over once again.

I jabbed him in the shoulder with my index finger and whispered, "Yes, *her* door was open. . .but *ours* was not. How did Spike get out of *our* room into hers?"

"He probably snuck out when you came to bed, Annie," Warren said. "But it doesn't matter. What's done is done. Let's just get some sleep and talk about it tomorrow." He rolled back over, and within seconds I heard his steady breathing.

How could he sleep? I knew in my gut that Spike hadn't knocked that candle over. He'd only gone into her room later. . .after the fact. And since when did Opal light a candle at night before bed? I'd never even noticed a candle in the room before. I certainly hadn't given it to her. And I hadn't purchased it when I bought the lace curtains and mirror she'd insisted upon.

Leaning back against the pillow, I tried to make sense of this. The more I thought about it, the more I realized. . . we might very well have a white-haired pyromaniac on our hands.

Under our *roof*, no less.

CHAPTER ⛩ NINE

MATCHMAKER, MATCHMAKER,
MAKE ME A MATCH

The following morning, after taking her walk and putting on her face, Opal headed off to the grocery store. I waited until she was gone to telephone Sergeant O'Henry. He agreed to meet me at my house and arrived minutes later with Molly O'Shea in tow.

Sasha met them at the door, growling as if they'd come to murder us all. Spike ran in crazy circles around O'Henry, even going so far as to lift his leg on the man's ankle. That went over well. And Copper. . .well, Copper rolled over on his back, begging for his tummy to be rubbed. Molly, who turned out to be a dachshund lover, was happy to oblige.

Off in the distance, Don Quixote howled from inside his crate. I'd grown used to the high-pitched wails, but O'Henry stuck his fingers in his ears and looked around, clearly shaken. "What is that?" he asked.

"Opal's cat."

"Ah. Say no more. I've met Don Quixote before." O'Henry looked around at my pups and shook his head. "You've got quite a menagerie going here, Annie. Thinking of opening a zoo or something?"

I could certainly see how he might think that but

responded with a brusque, "Hardly."

"Well, you'd better cut back on the critters. Clark County has a pet limit, you know."

"They do?" I'd never considered such a thing. "You're not going to write me up, are you?" He wouldn't dare. He'd be losing his best investigator!

"Funny. I just can't believe Warren is okay with all this."

O'Henry and the new deputy sat on the sofa opposite me as I filled them in. "I hate to say this, but Opal has been behaving. . .suspiciously."

"More than usual?" O'Henry flipped open his little notepad and reached for a pen. Turning to Molly, he added, "She walks her cat. On a leash."

"Ah." Molly nodded, her eyes narrowing as she took in this information. "Very strange."

"Stranger than you know." I quickly filled them in on the goings-on in the night. O'Henry's eyes narrowed when I told him about the fire.

"Annie, you should have called the fire department. I can't believe Warren didn't insist."

"No, it wasn't that kind of fire," I explained. "The candle just tipped over, and the wax dripped down the edge of the end table, leaving a little trail that ignited. Somehow the flames caught the edge of the comforter, but there was really very little damage except the smell of smoke. And, um. . . well, Opal has been asking for a new comforter anyway."

I hadn't remembered that little nugget till just now.

"So, what are you thinking?" O'Henry gave me a pensive look.

I leaned forward and whispered, "Have you given any

thought to the idea that she might've set her own place on fire to collect the insurance money? The building wasn't up to code, and I have my suspicions she didn't have the funds to *get* it up to code."

The good sergeant leaned back against the sofa and crossed his arms, never letting go of the little notebook and pen. "Well, of course. That's one angle. But we have no proof."

For the first time, I noticed that Molly's hand trembled as she wrote down the information. She looked up from her notepad with a dubious look in her eye. "She's just a lonely old woman. Right? What makes you think she might be capable of such devious behavior? Seems a little odd to me that folks are pointing fingers at her, all things considered. She's had a rough go of it."

"Right, but. . .I. . .I don't know." Drawing in a breath, I considered how this must sound to our new deputy. While I didn't want anyone to think ill of Opal, I had my reasons to suspect her. "She upped her policy just two weeks prior to the fire. What do you think of that?"

"I think it happens all the time," Molly said with a shrug. "Nothing terribly strange about adjusting your coverage."

O'Henry nodded in agreement. "I just adjusted my policy, too. We got a new big-screen TV last month, so I felt like more coverage was necessary. People up their insurance all the time, Annie."

"Yes, but get this. She had a candle in her room."

"You find that suspicious?" Molly asked, her green eyes catching my attention.

"Very."

"Maybe you wouldn't mind elaborating on that," she said.

I'd just started to do so when the front door opened and Spike shot outside.

"Oh not again!" I rose to my feet to chase after him.

My son's voice rang out. "Don't worry, Mom. I'll get him." He entered the room seconds later with Spike squirming in his arms. "What do you think you're doing, you little mutt?" Devin paused when he saw we had guests, his jaw dropping a bit as he noticed the redheaded beauty sitting before him.

"Devin, this is Molly O'Shea." I rose to my feet, and she joined me, giving him a shy glance.

I'd seen my son awestruck before, but never like this. He put the dog down and stared. Stared. Now, I'd taught the boy that staring was impolite, but it appeared he couldn't seem to help himself. He finally managed a shaky, "G—good to m—meet you."

Molly blushed. Blushed. *Goodness. First Teresa and Elio, now Molly and Devin? Is there something in the air? Maybe Opal's sprayed some sort of air freshener with matchmaking qualities.*

"They're here because, well, Opal's been acting a little odd." I shrugged, unsure of what to say next.

Devin quirked a brow. "How would you know?"

We all had a good laugh at that one, and the tension in the air seemed to release like air from an overinflated balloon.

"I, um. . .I'll be in the kitchen," Devin stammered. "I just came by to. . ." He couldn't seem to remember why he'd come by.

"To pick up your cell phone?" I prompted. "You left it here last night after dinner."

"Right. Yeah." He backed out of the room, nodding at

O'Henry and staring all the while at our new guest. The boy had never been very good at keeping his emotions hidden, but right now it didn't seem to be working against him. Molly gave him a shy smile and then shifted her gaze to the carpet.

We turned our attention back to the topic at hand. I offered my suspicions and shared every detail of last night's fire. O'Henry seemed to shrug off most of my speculations, but Molly—to her credit—kept her pen moving across her pad, jotting down everything I said.

I like this girl. She's really organized. Has it all together. And she smiled at my son. "Hmm." My mind began to reel at the possibilities.

"So you think Opal purchased the candle with the intention of setting the room on fire?" Molly asked with a worried look in her eye.

"Well, I don't know. Just seems suspicious, is all."

Opal chose that moment to enter the house singing, "Matchmaker, Matchmaker, make me a match."

The pen in Molly's hand slipped to the floor, and she scrambled to pick it up, her hands now visibly trembling. *Man, this girl is new on the job. She's a nervous wreck.*

"Oh Annie!" Opal's voice rang out after singing another line or two of her little ditty. "I went shopping!" She entered the room, her arms full of packages, but stopped cold when she saw O'Henry. At once, tension filled the air. Gone was her happy-go-lucky song. This Opal was a different beast altogether, one with fear—or was that *distrust*—in her eyes.

She nodded curtly at the sergeant then muttered, "I'll just drop these off in the kitchen and head to my room. I'm feeling a nap coming on."

Very odd.

I took note of the fact that Molly paled at Opal's entrance. *What's up with that?* Everything about the girl's countenance changed. Very suspicious.

Opal had no sooner made it to the far side of the living room than Devin joined us once again. "Would anyone like coffee?" he asked, looking only at Molly. "I'm about to make some."

"Sure," O'Henry said with a shrug. "I'll take a cup."

Devin nodded but never even looked O'Henry's way. No, my son's eyes were fixed on a pretty little deputy with red hair and freckles.

Molly smiled. "I don't really need the caffeine, but I guess a little won't hurt."

Opal stopped cold, looking back and forth between Devin and Molly. Back and forth. Back and forth. I could almost read her mind. "Oy, do we have a match here, or what?"

To her credit, she said nothing. Instead, she gave O'Henry another sour look then turned on her heel and headed off to her room.

In that moment, a thought occurred to me. Perhaps Opal had multiple personality disorder. One moment she could be as sweet as could be—matching up happy couples—and the next. . .well, the next, she was snapping people's heads off and setting rooms on fire. My insides turned to mush as I thought through the possibility of "Good Opal" and "Bad Opal." Of course, she'd proven herself more bad than good.

With a shiver, I turned back to O'Henry and Molly O'Shea.

The good sergeant's words encapsulated my thoughts exactly. He leaned my way and whispered, "Looks like Annie Peterson has met her match. . .in an elderly matchmaker."

Yep. Truer words ne'er were spoken.

CHAPTER ❚❚❘❘❘ TEN

AFTER THE FIRE IS GONE

On Saturday morning, I decided a trip to the Liberty Belle was in order. Candy, a resident beautician, had been after me to trim my hair. I needed to look my best for Louise's upcoming wedding, after all, and I needed the distraction from everything going on at home.

As I drove through town, I paused in front of the charred remains of Opal's business. Something told me to circle the building. I made a right in front of the cell phone store and did just that. As I came around to the back of what had been The Perfect Match, I paused a moment, even going so far as to pull the car over to the curb.

Hmm. The cell phone store. I'd read in the paper that they'd upped their security a couple of months back after a break-in. Maybe their cameras covered the street outside the store. If so, perhaps there was some sort of physical evidence from the morning of the fire. I'd have to pass that little tidbit off to O'Henry. In the meantime, my hair needed tending to. Shifting the car into DRIVE, I headed off to the salon. After that, I needed to stop off at our local supercenter to pick up a new comforter for Opal's bed. She'd requested blue. Not bright blue or sky blue, mind you, but a nice shade of ice blue. Go figure.

I arrived at our small-town beauty shop, surprised to find it so empty. Usually the place was hopping on a Saturday morning. This particular morning, I noticed only one other customer—Kathy Brewster. Interesting. A divine appointment, perhaps?

"Hey, Mom!" Candy approached, a smile on her face. "You made it! Opal didn't hog-tie you to the oven or force you to take her to the mall?"

"No." I sighed then gestured for Candy to lower her voice. "She's not as bad as I've made her out to be, honey. And I'm really, really working on guarding my tongue so I don't gossip about her."

"Mom, she's *worse* than you've made her out to be. And she gives us way too much stuff to talk about." Candy laughed as she raised her hands in mock defeat. "But I'll do my best to guard my tongue, too. I've got to believe the Lord has a greater plan here. Maybe He's preparing us all for something."

"Armageddon?" I offered.

Candy laughed until she had tears streaming down her face. "Maybe." Her expression softened and she dabbed at her eyes. "Or maybe we're all supposed to be setting an example for Opal. Ya know? She's not a believer, is she?"

"No." I sighed. Much as I'd hoped to set an example of godliness and Christian charity, my witness had flown out the window the night of the fire. "I don't know, Candy. I'm trying. But pray for me if you think of it. I can use all the support I can get."

"I have been praying, I promise. But this isn't something

you can do in your own strength, Mom," Candy said as she slipped a cape around me. "The Bible's pretty clear on that." She paused before adding, "On a completely different note, you know you've made the headlines in the paper, right?"

"W–what?"

She handed me the *Clark County Gazette,* and I read the headline on the front page: CLARKSBOROUGH FACES SECOND BLAZE IN LESS THAN A WEEK. Underneath the headline, Chris Brewster had used the church's latest headshot of Warren and me.

"What in the world?" I looked up at Candy, stunned, and then lowered my voice so that Kathy wouldn't hear me. "I can't believe he did this."

"I thought maybe you'd given him the information or something," Candy said with a shrug. "Couldn't figure out why you'd do that, though."

"No." I pursed my lips, deep in thought. "But I'll bet I know who did."

"Opal?"

"Yeah." But why would she do that? To draw attention away from the fire at her shop or to somehow make me look bad?

"Read the whole article, Mom. It's pretty interesting."

I zipped through it, stopping cold at the details about the tipped-over candle. Whoever had given this information to Chris had been thorough. Detailed.

"It's got to be Opal," I said, pointing at the text. "Look at this part: 'A small Maltese is to blame for the fire.' "

"Oh man." Candy shook her head. "Brandi's going to have a fit when she reads that."

"I'm having a little trouble with it myself. Still haven't figured out how Spike got in her room. Or if he had anything to do with the fire at all. Oh, but did you read the rest?" I asked. "Says right here that police suspect arson at Opal's place."

"Well, we'd already heard that through the rumor mill," Candy said. "But I guess it's official now."

"Maybe Opal's a suspect," I whispered. "Maybe that's why Chris ran this article, to see if folks would make the connection."

Candy's mouth formed a perfect O as her eyes widened. "Mom, you've got to get her out of your house."

"Not yet. My work isn't done. There's a lot to figure out."

"Yeah, like, 'Will my marriage survive a crazy old lady living in my house?'" Candy laughed. "How does Dad feel about this?" She gave me a motherly look, and I cringed.

"Oh you know your father. He's cool with my. . . investigations." Shifting my gaze, I hoped she'd change the direction of the conversation. To be quite honest, I'd been more than a little concerned about how Warren was taking all this. Poor guy. I'd put him through so much over the years.

"Mm-hmm. But I'll bet he's not so cool with the house burning down."

"Probably not." I decided a change in subject was in order. "We should get this trim over with. I've got a full day ahead of me."

"Okay." Candy gestured to the row of sinks at the back of the salon. "We can finish talking about it while I shampoo your hair."

"No way. I came here to wash this mess right out of my hair. So let's avoid the subject, okay?"

"You've got it."

I took a seat in the chair and leaned back. This was always my favorite part. I never considered washing my own hair a luxury, but there was something about the feel of a beautician's nails against a weary scalp that always seemed to relax me. I rested and enjoyed the experience as Candy kept talking.

"Just one more thing, Mom, and then I'll let it go. Garrett and I have been talking about this. And if you're really at your wit's end, Spike can come and stay at our place. Garrett is working from home quite a bit these days, and I can adjust my schedule to take the dog out every few hours when he's at the office."

"Really?" I released a sigh as I thought about her offer.

She shrugged. "I'm not saying it'll be easy. We're both working long hours, and I've been so exhausted lately. But if you really need us. . ."

I paused, taking in the weariness in my daughter's eyes. "That's a nice offer, honey, but I hate to give up so quickly. Couldn't I just send Opal to you instead?" I offered a playful smile, and Candy splattered my cheek with the foamy shampoo.

"No way! I might be generous, but I'm not *that* generous!"

She finished shampooing and conditioning my hair then wrapped a towel around my head and put me in an upright position.

As I settled into her chair, I took note of Kathy in the seat next to mine. She flashed a smile as Bonnie—the other beautician—styled her hair in one of those really cute, trendy bobs that's a little longer in the front than the back. So many women in our community were getting that haircut that Sheila and I had started calling it the "Clarksborough Do." With my rounder face, I'd already decided it would be a "don't" on me, so I stuck with my usual, shorter bob.

Bonnie finished up and walked to the register to take Kathy's payment then headed to the back room, muttering something about needing to throw some towels in the dryer and sweep the floor.

Kathy took a few steps in my direction and faced me with a strained smile. "What do you think of my hair, Annie? I've been dying to do this for ages, but I didn't know what Chris would say." Right away, her smile faded.

I reached to pat her hand. "I think he'd be crazy not to love it. You're gorgeous, and that new haircut just brings out your beauty even more."

"Really?" Her eyes misted over. "I'm trying, Annie." She lowered her voice. "I'm really trying to be everything he wants me to be. Everything Opal said he wanted in a wife."

Ah ha. Bingo. I'd wondered how long we would be together before the "O word" came up in conversation.

"Opal said I was his perfect match," Kathy whispered. "But I'm not so sure anymore. Maybe the woman I was trying to be while we were dating doesn't really exist. Ya know? Maybe it was all just pretense."

I nodded, though I couldn't quite connect with her words, at least on a personal level. Warren had always shown me such unconditional love; it was hard to imagine having to work to please him.

Candy stopped fidgeting with my hair for a moment and then mumbled something about a phone call she needed to make. I'd have to remember to thank her later. Clearly Kathy needed to talk—privately. Candy turned on her heel, leaving my wet hair piled atop my head.

"Kathy, listen. . ." I gazed into her eyes, hoping I could make sense of my thoughts. "You are beautiful inside and out. And you're a godly woman, someone who loves the Lord with her whole heart. That makes you extra beautiful. Maybe you worked too hard to please Chris while you were dating—I don't know—but that doesn't mean you have to lose sight of the real you."

"What if he doesn't like the real me?" she whispered. "The real me is a little messy sometimes, and I don't really like to cook. At least not every night. I work double time to prove to myself—and to Chris—that I'm the woman he wants, but I'm just wearing myself out. Sometimes I want to let my guard down, to just be myself. Is that asking too much?"

"No. And this isn't as unusual as you think," I assured her. "Everyone goes through this during the honeymoon phase. It starts with that first night, when all of your physical flaws are bared. And it just continues from there. If Chris is the man I think he is"—*Dear God, let him be the man I think he is*—"he will love you, flaws and all. And vice versa." I leaned in to whisper the rest. "And did it ever occur to you that he might be working overtime to prove something to you, too? Maybe he's so unsure of himself that he's putting on a show when you're around. Sometimes men are like that."

She leaned back in her chair and sighed. "Not Chris. I've

never met anyone more sure of himself. Look at what he's done with the *Gazette*. Circulation has never been higher. Oh, speaking of which. . ." She snapped her fingers. "Did you hear the news about Janetta?"

"What news?"

Kathy beamed. "She got picked to be on that Super Chef show."

"No way! I knew she was auditioning, but I had no idea she'd actually made it onto the show."

"Yes. Turns out one of the other contestants had to cancel at the last minute, so they called her. She's elated. Keep your eye out for the headline on that story."

"I'm sure Chris got a kick out of that one."

"Oh yes." A dreamy expression came over her. "He's really good at what he does, Annie. Chris has turned that paper around. In less than three years, no less. And he always catches the headlines before anyone else in this part of the state. He's a tough reporter."

No joke. So tough he elaborates on gossip and capitalizes on people's pain.

"I'd be willing to wager he's not so tough on the inside. I've known a few men like Chris who work overtime to prove themselves publicly but are really a mess on the inside." I paused a minute then asked a hard question. "I know you're a believer, and I know Chris attends church on Sundays. . . but do you have any idea where he stands with the Lord?"

She shook her head, and more tears tipped her lashes. "Annie, that's just it. I've never seen any indication that he has a walk with the Lord other than his church attendance. I can't believe I'm actually saying that out loud, but it's true.

And sometimes. . ." She shook her head and whispered, "Sometimes I think the only reason he goes to church at all is to get the latest scoop on people."

"He's looking for the next headline. . .at church?" I asked.

"Yeah, and he's found it a couple times. Remember that story about corruption in the mayor's office?"

"Oh, right." The article had left a lasting impression, and several jobs had been lost as a result of the things Chris had turned up.

"He got his information from Jon Goodman, chairman of the missions committee at church. Jon works—or rather, worked—for the mayor. He also happens to like coffee, so Chris makes sure he's always got the brand Jon likes."

"Ah."

"Maybe I shouldn't be telling you all of this," she said, her gaze shifting to make sure we weren't overheard. "But I don't have anyone to talk to. Not really."

"You should call Evelyn." I nodded as I mentioned our pastor's wife. The woman was a wealth of wisdom. "And don't discount the power of an awesome God. He's got the ability to heal your marriage."

"I know." Kathy drew in a breath. "And that's my prayer. But you have to have two willing parties, you know? And I'm just so afraid Chris has settled into this complacency mode where our marriage is concerned. He's far too busy with his career now. That paper means the world to him. And I'm just. . .I don't know." Tears began to flow at this point. "Annie, I'm thirty-nine. Thirty-nine."

"Okay." *I'm not sure what that has to do with anything, but I'll let her finish.*

"I want to have a baby. . .before it's too late."

"Ah. I see."

"But I'm just not sure bringing a child into this environment is for the best, and that breaks my heart."

She began to cry in earnest now, and I reached to take her hand. What could I possibly say to make things better? "Kathy, I have to confess, I don't have any answers for you. And I'm scared to speculate, because I might say the wrong thing. But I know Someone who does have the answers, and I think we need to ask Him for His input. Do you mind if I pray?"

"Of course not!"

It felt a little odd, bowing my head in the Liberty Belle, but I did it anyway. I didn't have to go looking for passion to put behind these words. No, it came naturally. I'd heard enough about Chris Brewster in one day to muster up plenty of gumption to pray. Pouring out my heart, I asked the Lord for His mercy over this situation and for His favor in the Brewsters' marriage. Several times I felt Kathy squeeze my hand. And when I finished with a strong "Amen," I opened my eyes to find tears streaming down her face.

"Thank you, Annie." She reached to hug me. "You're the only one I know who would stop in the middle of a public place and pray for a friend."

"Really?" I pondered that a moment. "Well, I'll tell you why I do it. Came from something Evelyn said in Bible study a couple of years ago. She said, 'Next time, instead of telling someone you're going to be praying for them, just stop right then and there and do it.' I never forgot her words." Chuckling, I added, " 'Course, the first time was a little awkward. Happened in the ladies' room at a Chinese restaurant. But I've discovered that just about anyplace can be turned into a prayer closet. As long as two or more are gathered together. Ya know?"

"I know." She flashed a hopeful smile. "And I'm so grateful to you, Annie. I need someone like you in my life—someone who has a great, healthy marriage. I aspire to be in a marriage like yours."

At once my thoughts flew back to what Candy had said: *How does Dad feel about this?*

Hmm. I hadn't really included Warren as much as I should have, had I? Maybe, before I started advertising the strength of my marriage, I'd better spend a little time working on it.

Candy chose that moment to return, and Kathy said her good-byes. As my daughter trimmed my hair, my thoughts gravitated to Warren. He'd put up with so much over the past few years, hadn't he? What other husband would encourage his wife to get involved in so many investigations? Was he secretly seething? Wishing I'd give this up, once and for all? Should I? *Hmm.* One more thing to pray about.

I was thankful that Candy distracted me with conversation about Louise and Nick's upcoming wedding. From there, our conversation shifted to the fact that her feet hurt—Candy's not Louise's. That led us to a conversation about how Candy needed to take it easy, not work so many hours. This conversation, of course, also convinced me that Candy and Garrett did not need to be taking care of Spike. They already had enough going on.

When she finished my hair, I stared in the mirror with a smile. "A good haircut always makes me feel better."

"I know. It's like a new lease on life, isn't it? A new beginning. A fresh start."

"Well, I don't know that I would take it that far, but I do feel better." I examined my appearance in the mirror, sighing as I observed the crow's feet around my eyes. If I wanted to go on feeling better, I should look away from the mirror.

I thanked Candy for her work, paid her, left a generous tip, and then scooted out of the shop. As I did, several troubling thoughts rolled through my brain. I'd known Kathy and Chris's marriage was rocky, sure. But this rocky? My heart nearly broke for the poor woman. Right then and there, I made a commitment to pray for them—daily.

My thoughts shifted to Chris's most recent newspaper headline. Why would Opal have given him that information for the newspaper? Wouldn't she have realized he'd turn it against her, making her look like a suspect? And why would she have mentioned the dog, of all things? A dead giveaway that she'd ratted us out!

As I opened the door to the car, another idea occurred to me. Why hadn't I thought of this before? There was someone else who could have given the information to Chris Brewster. Someone I knew very little about. Someone whose hand had trembled as she'd scribbled the information into her notepad.

Molly O'Shea.

Hadn't I given her all the details about the fire less than twenty-four hours ago? And what did we really know about the fiery redhead, anyway? No one in town seemed to be connected to her, did they? No, she was a total stranger to us. What if she'd taken the information I'd shared and. . .

My thoughts whirled as I contemplated the possibilities.

Why? Why would she do that?

Looked like I was in this thing up to my eyeballs. No turning back now! If I wanted to match my son with the lovely Molly O'Shea, I had to clear her name first!

CHAPTER ELEVEN

BLOWING IN THE WIND

As I left the beauty parlor, I tried to absorb all I'd heard from Kathy. Chris was working double time to make his paper number one. No big news there. Every newspaper editor wanted to be number one. . .if he was worth his weight in salt.

I pondered these tidbits of information as I made the drive home. I'd no sooner pulled into the driveway than my cell phone rang. I glanced down, surprised to see Sheila's number.

"Hey, I thought you and Orin were in New York this week," I said upon answering.

"Well, hello to you, too." She sighed. "We're in New York, but it's not much of a trip. Orin's here on business, and I'm stuck in a hotel room."

"Really? You're not shopping? I figured you'd hit every department store in Manhattan. Twice. Or three times."

"Did that yesterday, and I'm—" She sneezed. "Coming down with a cold. So, I had to resort to spending the day in the hotel room."

"Weird. Everyone here is feeling under the weather, too."

"Well you know what they say. Summer colds are the

worst." She dissolved into a coughing fit. When she caught her breath, she said, "I'm really just calling to see how it's going with Opal. A little birdie told me she's wreaking havoc."

"She's a piece of work, Sheila. I'm really rethinking my decision to bring her into our home, especially with the wedding in eight days."

"Evelyn called," Sheila said. "Told me she's worried about you. Said she ran into you at the supermarket and you looked exhausted. And I hear you've made the headlines. Something about a fire."

"Yes." I sighed. "We're fine. Well, the house is fine anyway. But I can't figure out for the life of me who leaked the information to Chris."

"Humph."

"I know. It's probably Opal. In fact, I think I might be on to something. Listen to this." I told her about finding my houseguest with the matches in her hand and her head in the oven. Then I talked her through the details of the fire in the bedroom, honing in on the part about the dog.

"It is a little strange," Sheila admitted. "I mean, one minute we're talking about whether or not Opal might've burned down her business to get the insurance money, and the next thing we know, she's holding matches and setting your bedroom on fire."

"Devin's bedroom, if we're going to get technical about it. And I guess it's possible the dog knocked over the candle, though I can't figure out how he got out of my room. Oh, and speaking of Devin. . ." I went on to tell her about Molly's visit and my son's flabbergasted response upon meeting her.

"So, you think they're a match?" Sheila asked.

"Maybe. Can't really say how she responded to him. I was too busy watching Devin trip all over himself to wait on her."

"Now, that's the boy I know and love," Sheila said. "And if anyone deserves a good woman, he does." After a pause, she added, "What do you know about Molly anyway?"

"Ugh. You had to ask."

"What?" The tone of her voice changed immediately.

"I don't know anything about her. And I. . .well, I've actually been a little suspicious that *she* might've given that information to Chris. If Opal didn't, I mean."

"No way." Sheila laughed. "Annie, this is nuts! We're in our menopausal years. We shouldn't be worrying about who burned down what. We should be going on cruises and talking about hot flashes. Wearing red hats and sipping Earl Grey tea."

"We can still do all of that, trust me. Though I'd rather talk about going on another missions trip, not a cruise."

"Ooo, me, too. I'm hoping we can get to Nicaragua before the year is out. Evelyn's working on that."

Just then, I noticed a car driving slowly past my house. Glancing in the rearview mirror gave me the perfect view. Yes, the silver SUV definitely slowed its pace in front of my house, but why? And why did the driver pause to stare?

"Sheila. . ." I watched as the driver put the vehicle in reverse and backed up to my driveway, "I have to go."

"What's up?"

"I'm not sure." A shiver wriggled down my spine as I added, "Someone is here. I'll call you back later and fill you in. But pray, okay? I'm feeling a little overwhelmed."

"Will do."

We ended the call, and I shoved my cell phone into my purse before getting out of my car. By then, the fellow in the SUV had pulled into my driveway alongside me. He swung his car door open and offered me a smile. "I'm looking for an Opal Lovelace."

"Ah, she's inside."

With a brusque nod, he exited his car and took a few steps in my direction. "I'm Dennis Robbins, an adjuster with Farmers Mutual Insurance Company out of Philadelphia."

"Oh, of course." A wave of relief washed over me. Finally. The sooner the insurance company settled with Opal, the sooner she could get back to rebuilding. Or finding a new place to live.

I led him inside the house, where we were greeted with Opal's voice raised in anger. "I told you to get away from me, you stupid dog! I don't want you climbing all over me. I'm not a. . ." She looked up just in time to see us, shame washing over her face. "Oh, hi Annie."

"Opal." I mustered up a strained smile for the sake of the insurance agent. "You have a guest."

Mr. Robbins extended his hand. "Ms. Lovelace, I'm Dennis Robbins with Farmers Mutual Insurance Company."

"Well, it's about time you showed up," she muttered. "C'mon in here and let's get this over with so you can cut me a check."

His brow wrinkled as he followed her into the living room, briefcase in hand.

"Mr. Robbins, would you like a cup of coffee or maybe a glass of water or something?"

"Oh, no thank you." He flashed a smile. "I'm fine."

At my gesture, he settled onto the sofa and opened his briefcase, pulling out a stack of papers and an ink pen. Opal took a seat in the chair next to the sofa, Don Quixote in hand.

"I'll just scoot on out of here and give you two some privacy," I offered.

"No, Annie." Opal looked at me, a pleading look in her eyes. "I want you to stay. I might need you."

"Okay." I looked at the adjuster. "Is that all right?"

"Fine with me if it's fine with her." He shrugged as he turned to face Opal. "First, let me apologize for coming on the weekend. I've been swamped with work, and I'm just getting over a little cold." He pulled a handkerchief from his pocket and squeezed his nose. Right away, Opal shifted back in her seat and began to fan herself, muttering, "Is everyone on the planet sick right now?"

"I've already gone by your place and taken photographs," Mr. Robbins said. "And I'll be going by the fire department once we finish up here to speak to the investigator."

"Well, that's good," Opal said. "I'm glad to hear you're finally doing something."

"Mm-hmm." To the adjuster's credit, he held his tongue. "Tell me every detail of what happened the morning of the fire, Ms. Lovelace."

"I was having my breakfast, as always." She gave him a scrutinizing glance. "Do you need to know what I was eating?"

"That won't be necessary."

"Oatmeal. I was eating oatmeal. Eat it every morning. Good for the heart."

"Ah." He gave her a pensive look and then scribbled something down.

"I always try to eat healthy. So many of the people I know these days are eating processed food products"—she stared at me—"but I'm a firm believer in eating right." She paused and appeared to be deep in thought. "Anyway, I was sitting there eating my oatmeal and drinking coffee when I smelled something suspicious."

"Smoke?"

"Hmm." She shrugged. "I smelled that, too, but this was a really strong odor, like at a gas station."

"So, gasoline?"

"Maybe. Some sort of chemical. Next thing you know, I hear this loud explosion, and I'm seeing stars. My back door blew in on me."

Mr. Robbins's face reflected his surprise at this news. "I'm so sorry this happened to you. Were you injured?"

"Well, my shoulder was hurt, but not bad. I was so busy hunting for Don Quixote in the seconds after the explosion that I don't remember the pain. Just remember everything feeling like a dream. I kept thinking I'd wake up."

"And then what happened?"

"Well, as I said, I was seeing stars, so everything from this point on got a little fuzzy. I remember there were flames inside the house and the smoke was really thick. So I did what they always tell you to do."

"Which is?"

"Grabbed the most important things and got the heck out of Dodge."

"What did you take?"

"My laptop," she explained. "I need it to keep my business up and running. Got nobody else to support me in my old age."

He scribbled a few words then looked up. "What else?"

"A box of old photographs. A handful of clothes from the top of the dryer and my purse."

"And the cat?" He scribbled all this information down.

"Of course." At this, Opal's eyes filled with tears. "I don't know what I'd do if I ever lost Don Quixote. He's the only family I've got."

I swallowed the lump in my throat, amazed at the tenderness in her voice. Now this was a side of Opal Lovelace I hadn't seen. A tender, gentle side.

Mr. Robbins picked up on this, and his tone softened. "I'm sorry for all you've been through. I'm sure it must've been really frightening."

"Scariest thing that's ever happened to me in eighty-three years, and I've been through a lot in my life!" She went on to tell him about outliving several husbands, and he nodded.

"Ms. Lovelace, I'm sorry to add to your pain, but we're going to need you to make a list of every item of any value that was in your house. Clothing. Appliances. Televisions, video players. Anything."

"Everything?" She shook her head. "Well for Pete's sake. Can't you just take my word for it?"

"Sorry, but if there's to be a reimbursement check of any kind, we're going to need a full accounting."

"What do you mean, *if*?" she asked, her lips tightening.

Mr. Robbins leaned forward in his chair, clicking his pen. "Well, as I mentioned before, we've already been in contact with the fire department by phone. And the police department, of course."

"So?"

"There's an arson investigation under way, Ms. Lovelace. You know, of course, that we can't release any funds to you until. . ." He scratched his head.

"Until what?" Opal crossed her arms.

"Until we know for sure what happened."

Her expression hardened immediately and her tone intensified. "So you're telling me I won't see a penny of my money till the fire marshal and that no-good deputy figure this out?" Opal rose and clutched the cat, which now began to hiss at Mr. Robbins. "This is ridiculous. What am I supposed to do till then?"

Mr. Robbins nodded in my direction. "Well, it looks like you've got the support of friends. If you can just go on staying here for a few weeks, maybe we'll get this thing sorted out."

The man flashed me a smile, but to be honest, he'd lost me at the words *a few weeks*. Everything after that was a blur.

CHAPTER ⫟⫟⫟ TWELVE

KEEP THE FLAME BURNIN'

Early Sunday morning, Opal returned from her usual three-mile walk, minus the cat. She didn't look particularly worried about the fact that her companion had gone missing, but I felt compelled to ask about him, anyway.

"Where's Don Quixote?" I queried as I scooped hearty servings of oatmeal into bowls.

My houseguest dismissed my words with the wave of a hand. "Oh, he's off on one of his quests. Conquering the world of female felines."

"Beg your pardon?" I took a seat at the table, reaching for the sugar bowl. If I had to eat oatmeal, I might as well doctor it up.

"He got away from me in the park. Nothing new there."

"Should we send out a posse?" Warren asked as he entered the room. "Go look for him?"

"No, he often goes off on these little adventures," she explained. "Sometimes he's gone for hours. I never worry about him."

"But he's in a new environment. You don't think he'll. . ." I didn't finish. No point in getting her worried. Still I had to wonder if the little guy would find his way home.

Opal headed off to her room and surprised me by showing up in the kitchen dressed in a different outfit just as I rinsed out our cereal bowls. I could tell she'd done a rush job with her makeup, because the eyeliner was cattywompus and the lipstick went far beyond the boundaries of her lips.

"Do you think this will do for church?" she asked, turning around to show off a somewhat worn-looking dress.

I did my best not to gasp aloud. Opal. . .going to church? Was I hearing things?

"You look great, honey," I said, trying to hold my voice steady. "And besides, folks these days don't pay much attention to who's wearing what. It's more 'Come as you are.' "

"Well, that's a switch from when I used to go to that church years ago. Back then it was all about who could outdo who with their latest dresses."

I was surprised to hear that Opal had ever attended Clarksborough Community Church. I'd never heard her mention it before, and I certainly didn't remember seeing her there in my younger years.

Warren and I scurried off to our room, dressing in record time.

"Don't want to give her time to change her mind," he said.

"I know! Can you believe she's going?" I smiled, pondering the what-ifs. "Maybe we're doing something right, Warren."

"Or maybe. . ." He pursed his lips, not finishing his sentence. I hate it when he does that.

"Maybe what?"

"I don't know." He shook his head. "Maybe I'm just overly suspicious where she's concerned, but I have to wonder if she's up to something."

"Hope not." I pondered his words as I touched up my hair and makeup. Did the elderly matchmaker have something up her sleeve? If so, what?

We left for church a few minutes later. Warren took his usual spot behind the wheel. I sat in the front and Opal sat in back. As we passed through town, I noticed she looked at the charred remains of her home with an exaggerated sigh. I couldn't blame her. The whole thing was terribly sad. And terribly odd. We still didn't have a clue who'd set The Perfect Match ablaze.

Thankfully, I didn't have time to think much about it before Warren pulled in the parking lot of the church. Minutes later, we exited the car. I whispered a silent prayer that all would go well. No point in adding to the ever-growing lump in my stomach, after all.

Sheila met us at the front door, wearing a new lime green pants and blouse ensemble. She spun in a circle. "What do you think, Annie? I bought it at Macy's in New York."

So much for telling Opal our church members don't try to outdo each other with their clothing choices anymore. "It's great, but. . .what happened?" I asked. "I thought you were staying in the Big Apple till Tuesday."

"Orin's meetings ended last night," she explained then sneezed. "So we decided to come on home because I'm not feeling well." As if for effect, she sneezed again.

"Please keep your distance, then," Opal said, taking a giant step backward. As she did, she accidentally bumped into a woman in a blue dress.

"Oh I'm sorry, I. . ." The woman turned, and I saw it was

Teresa Klein. This should be interesting.

"Well, isn't this a fine kettle of fish." Opal crossed her arms. "Here I go, breaking my vow never to come to this church again, and who do I run into first?" She pursed her lips and shook her head. "Wouldn't have taken you for a churchgoer, Teresa."

"Why not?" Teresa's voice sounded strained.

Yikes. Were we going to have a catfight right here on the front porch of Clarksborough Community Church?

"You insisted I give your money back." Opal clucked her tongue. "And heaven knows your timing really stinks, especially with all I'm going through. . ." She sucked in a breath and then continued. "And after all I did for you, trying to find the perfect match." Opal shook her head. "It's not my fault you were so picky. Lower your standards a little, and you might just find yourself a man."

As irony would have it, Louise, Nick, and Elio chose that minute to arrive. Elio took one look at Teresa and immediately gravitated to her side, his eyes lit with joy and anticipation. Talk about a well-timed moment.

"Good morning, lovely lady." He took her hand and kissed it. "We meet again. I've missed you terribly since our last meeting, and here you are!"

Teresa turned all kinds of red and whispered a shy, "Good morning, Elio. It's nice to see you again, too."

Opal watched this interaction in stunned silence. Oh, if only I could have read her thoughts!

Seconds later, Teresa shifted her attention from Elio back to Opal. With a forced smile, she managed a few strained words. "Opal, in light of everything you've been through. . .

and in light of God's goodness in my life, I believe I'll just drop the matter we were discussing. There will be no need to return any funds, and I do apologize for inconveniencing you with the idea in the first place. Please forgive me."

Well, if that didn't beat all. Was I witnessing Christian charity or an act of some sort? Hard to tell in this strange out-of-body experience I was having.

Thank goodness, Chris and Kathy Brewster chose that moment to appear. Of course, my thoughts shifted at once to everything Kathy had shared at the salon, but I kept those things to myself. Still, I had a hard time looking at Chris without wanting to deck him.

Chris nodded at Opal and muttered a brusque, "G'morning," before he walked on into the church.

Kathy paused and gently placed her hand on Opal's arm. "How are you getting along, Opal? Do you need anything?"

"I'm doing pretty well, in spite of everything I've been through." She sighed. "But I do wish I had some more clothes. I only managed to snag a handful of things when the fire broke out, and I haven't been shopping since."

Why hadn't I thought of that? Hadn't I heard Opal tell the insurance adjuster she'd only grabbed a few clothes? I could have—*should* have—taken her shopping for some new things.

"Well, I'd be happy to see to that," Kathy said, beaming. "You just leave it to me."

"You're a wonderful Christian woman," Opal said. "Unlike a few others I've known." She shifted her gaze to Teresa, her expression hardening.

"Oh, it's the least I can do," Kathy said. "You've always

been such an encouragement to Chris. And to me, too, of course. And with everything you're going through, the body of Christ needs to support you."

"Oh well, let's don't involve the church." Opal stared up at the steeple as the church bells played a lively hymn. "They don't owe me anything."

"It's not a matter of anyone owing anything," Kathy explained. "That's just what the church does. Cares for those in need. And you happen to be in need right now. Nothing shameful about that."

"Mm-hmm."

Just then, an elderly church member—Roger Kratz—met us at the door with his hand extended. I'd met Roger during one of my prior investigations. Poor fellow lost his wife over three years ago. He'd found a new home at the church, though, taking over the greeters' ministry and even helping out in the nursery on occasion.

Roger paused to give Opal a smile. "Good morning." He shook her hand, lingering a bit longer than I would have expected as he gazed into her eyes. "Welcome."

"Morning." She gave him an interested glance then turned back to me and muttered, "Maybe it won't be so bad here after all."

We followed along behind the crowd entering the building. Warren led the way to our pew. He shuffled in first. I followed, then Opal joined me. She looked around the room, a pained expression on her face.

"You okay?" I asked.

"Mm-hmm." She sucked in a breath then released it. "Just haven't been in here since I buried my last husband all those years ago. They've updated the place since then. And they have a new pastor. I saw his name on the sign outside. Pastor Miller."

"Yes, and he has a wonderful wife named Evelyn. I'm sure a lot of things have changed since you were here last." I reached to squeeze her hand.

She shrugged and continued to look around the room. "Seems like a mighty big waste, all of that stained glass. And I don't remember the pulpit being quite so ornate. A little too high and mighty, to my way of thinking. Churches don't need to be so show-offish." She began to mutter under her breath, but I couldn't make out her words.

"Never thought about it before." No, in fact I'd always thought the sanctuary was quite beautiful. Strange that Opal saw things so differently.

She pointed across the room to Chris and Kathy. After a contented sigh, she added, "I still think they make such a handsome couple. Don't you?"

"They look lovely together." *Better leave it at that.*

The rest of my family arrived in short order, and getting everyone seated took a couple of minutes. Well, all but Devin. Just about the time I thought he'd decided to play hooky, I saw him enter. . .with Molly O'Shea. I did a double take, thinking maybe I was hallucinating.

No, sure enough, Devin and Molly took their seats in the row in front of us, next to Sheila and Orin. This certainly got Opal's attention. She elbowed me and whispered, "I saw that one coming, just so you know. Couldn't have pegged it better myself."

Yes, I saw it coming, as well. But there were no match-making fees attached, unless the Lord decided to send a bill. I paused to think about Molly. Sure, she was in church, but where did she stand with the Lord? I thought about something our pastor had said once about how going to church didn't make you a Christian any more than standing in your garage made you a car. *Hmm.* Before matching Molly up with my son, I'd better make sure she'd already been matched up with the Almighty.

The music started, so our conversation came to its rightful conclusion. I could see the surprise in Opal's eyes as the drummer and guitar player entered the stage.

"What is this, a rock-and-roll show?" she asked. "Has Elvis come back or something?"

I shook my head, trying not to laugh. A few notes into the first song, Opal pressed her fingers in her ears and mouthed the word *loud.*

Really? I'd never thought about it before, but the added instruments probably were a little louder than she was accustomed to.

We rose to sing the first few songs, but Opal remained seated. I didn't blame her. At her age, all the up and down movement was likely hard on the joints. But at one point, in the middle of the song "Amazing Love," I turned back to give her a glance and noticed tears in her eyes. *Lord, You know better than any of us what Opal needs. Meet her where she is, Father. And help me be the kind of friend she needs—no more and no less.*

When the song service ended, Pastor Miller approached the podium and opened his Bible. "I'm going to be speaking from the gospel of Luke," he said. "The story of the good Samaritan."

As he shared the story of the man who'd been left for dead on the side of the road, I couldn't help but think of Opal. Like that man, she had no one to care for her, no one to meet her needs. Oh I'd been tempted to ignore her plight, like the passersby in the story, but God had stopped me. That wasn't to say I was thrilled that He'd stopped me, but—for whatever reason—I was the chosen party. Now, if only I could do the right thing. With the right attitude.

I ate up every word of the sermon, thankful Pastor Miller had chosen this particular message for today. I definitely needed the encouragement to keep on keepin' on, where Opal was concerned.

Several times I noticed a bit of sniffling to my left. Was Opal feeling the weight of his message, or had she picked up a cold from one of the many people she'd been in contact with of late? I certainly hoped it was the former and not the latter.

When the service ended, Warren turned my way. "I have to stay after for a quick meeting with the men's group. We're planning our yearly fishing trip. Do you mind waiting, or do you want to go on to the restaurant?"

"Oh, we'll wait. I don't mind a bit." Leaning close, I whispered, "Besides, I'm hoping Opal will get acquainted with some of these people. Might help."

"Well, speaking of Opal. . ." He paused, looking to make sure she couldn't hear him. "I was sort of hoping to sneak away from her today. Do lunch alone, just you and me. Thought the kids could take Opal to lunch at one restaurant and you and I could go to another." He gave me a playful wink. "What do you say?"

"Oh honey, I don't know. . .I've been a little worried about Candy lately. She hasn't been feeling well. And Maddy's got the sniffles. I'm sure Opal won't even get in the car with her."

He groaned.

"I know, I know." While I appreciated his idea, I couldn't imagine the sort of trouble Opal might cause for the kids. And truly, it was the kids I was thinking of here, not Opal. I dove into a list of possible catastrophes that might take place if I left her to her own devices, and Warren sighed.

"Well, it was just an idea." He shrugged. "Maybe next week. But Annie. . ." He took my hand and gazed at me lovingly. "I miss you."

A lump rose in my throat as I kissed him on the cheek. "I miss you, too, Warren. And I won't let this go on too long, I promise." *Lord, help me make good on that promise. I don't want anything to interfere with my relationship with this man.*

He headed off to his meeting, and I joined Opal in the foyer. As we walked out of the church, she scooted off to talk to Chris and Kathy. I caught a glimpse of Louise standing alone on the far side of the parking lot. Seeing her without Nick at her side raised my curiosity. She happened to look my way, and I smiled and headed through the throng of people to chat with her.

"A penny for your thoughts," I said. Then I saw the look of concern in her red-rimmed eyes.

"I'm not sure today's the right day, Annie."

"Louise." I touched her arm. "Something going on?"

Her gaze darted across the parking lot to Nick and Elio, who were engaged in conversation. Then she turned back to me. "Um. . ."

"What is it?" I asked.

At once, her countenance changed. For a moment, I thought she might cry. "Things have been a little. . .*off.* . . since Elio arrived."

"Off? Is he trying to take over Nick's business or something?"

"No, nothing like that." She glanced back at the men once again, sighing aloud. "It's just. . .I don't think Elio likes me very much."

"What? Are you kidding me? What's not to like about Louise McGillicuddy?" I went into a lengthy list of her attributes, finally bringing a smile to her face.

"I knew I could count on you to cheer me up, Annie," she said. "You always manage to do that." She lowered her voice. "And maybe I'm just a little paranoid, but I overheard Elio talking to Nick about me yesterday at the restaurant. They didn't know I was there. They still don't know I heard anything."

"What was he saying?" I asked.

This time Louise's eyes did fill with tears. "Nick and Elio were estranged after their parents died. I think there was some bad blood between them. Something to do with the family's restaurant. I only know that I overheard Elio saying something about how he'd hoped Nick would move back to Greece to take over the restaurant there. And I have a feeling Nick is considering it, just to keep the peace."

"What?" I couldn't believe it. "Nick is part of our community here. And he loves this town. And you. He loves *you.*"

"I know." Louise sighed. "I'm guessing Elio just has his heart set on Nick marrying a Greek woman, living in Greece, working in the family restaurant, and raising Greek children. As you can see, I'm certainly not Greek."

"Oh, I don't know. McGillicuddy sounds Greek to me." I offered up a wink, and she smiled through her tears.

"You're sweet. And funny. But I guess I can see his side. My mother—God rest her soul—would have loved nothing better than for me to marry a good Irish boy. Problem is. . ." She turned back to Nick with a sigh. "I fell in love with a good *Greek* boy."

"Yes, you did," I said with a grin. "And he fell in love with you, too. There's no denying how the two of you feel about each other."

She shifted her attention back to me. "I love him, Annie. I love him so much it hurts. And I don't want anything to get in the way of that. Opal might've played a small role in connecting us, but I believe with all my heart that God is ultimately responsible for putting us together. We are perfect for each other, regardless of our backgrounds."

"Well, of course. And time will prove that. Just don't let anyone else's opinion get in the way. Promise?"

She nodded. "I'll do my best."

Deep in thought, I turned my gaze back to Nick and Elio. Surely this stranger from across the ocean wouldn't thwart my friend's wedding plans. Would he? I watched as Teresa gravitated to Elio's side, and he turned to her with a boyish grin.

Nah. Looked like Elio Petracca was far too preoccupied with a certain female to cause any damage.

Louise cleared her throat, and I looked her way once more. "There is one more thing, Annie. I know this is a lot to ask—and please feel free to say no—but I was wondering if you could watch Ruby for me while I'm on my honeymoon."

"W–watch Ruby?" Yikes! Her darling little dachshund—daughter of my own Sasha and Copper—was a sweet thing. But. . .

"I just can't see boarding her for that length of time," Louise said with tears in her eyes. "And she always has so much fun when we come to your house. You've got that big backyard and all. . . ."

"Yes I do." Double yikes. What would Warren say? First Opal and Don Quixote, then Spike, now Ruby?

"Let me talk to Warren, and I'll get back to you."

"Thanks so much, Annie. You're a lifesaver!"

As we ended our conversation, I whispered a prayer. "Goodness, Lord! How far are we going to have to go with this Good Samaritan thing?"

I turned back to look at Opal, who stood on the porch steps, talking to none other than Evelyn, our pastor's wife. For the first time in ages, I actually saw a smile on her face—Opal's, not Evelyn's. Evelyn always smiled.

"Lord, what are you up to?" I whispered. "Are you asking me to hang on a bit longer? Do you have a greater plan for Opal Lovelace?"

My heart swelled with joy at the very idea. Yes, surely the Lord would give me the grace and mercy necessary to get through a few more days—or weeks—with Opal Lovelace. In the meantime, I had a wedding to plan!

CHAPTER ⛩ THIRTEEN

LIAR, LIAR, PANTS ON FIRE

We arrived home from lunch around one thirty. I was dying to ask Opal what she thought of the church service but didn't dare. Surely the topic would come up later. Right now, she looked happy to be home.

So did Warren. In fact, he'd looked a little out of sorts all day. I watched as he led the way to the front door, keys in hand. He chatted as he walked but stopped cold just short of the door. "What do we have here?"

"What is it, honey?"

He pointed, and I looked down at the doormat then gasped. "A. . .a mouse?" I stared at the dead rodent. "Who would do such a thing? Do you think someone is trying to tell us something?"

"Like what?" Warren asked, giving me a funny look.

"Maybe they think I'm ratting them out by investigating the fire?" My hands began to tremble as I thought about the possibilities.

"Oh Annie." Opal slapped me on the back then reached down and scooped up the dead mouse by the tail. Dangling it from her fingertips, she said, "This is a present from Don Quixote. He's always bringing me mice and birds and such.

It's his way of saying he loves me."

"Don Quixote?" Putting a dead mouse on someone's doorstep showed you loved them? Man, did I have a lot to learn about love!

Just then I heard a familiar mewing sound. So, the wanderer had returned home at last. He'd captured his prey, offered it as a sacrifice on my doormat, and now crooned with delight.

"Oh, Don Q! You're home." Opal tossed the dead mouse into the bushes, and I groaned. *Why did she do that? It's going to stink to high heaven.*

"I'll bury it later," Warren whispered. "You just tend to her."

Opal leaned down and scratched the cat behind the ears. "Were you off on another adventure, baby? You'll have to tell Mommy all about it. We're going to take a nap together, but I have plenty of time for a story. You just tell me about all of the neighboring villages you conquered, and I'll tell you my story about the fascinating people I met at that church they made me go to this morning."

Well, I guess that answers that.

Opal entered the house, muttering something under her breath about her keys.

"Everything okay?" I asked.

"I don't know." Her brow wrinkled—more than usual. "I could've sworn I had my keys with me this morning." She shrugged and headed off to her room. All along the way, I heard her talking to the cat. "I miss you when you go away, but I know it's never for long. You always come back to me.

I can count on you. Now, if only those silly keys would turn up as quickly as you!" She then went on talking about the list she needed to put together for the insurance company. Finally, her voice trailed off.

The eeriest feeling came over me—in part because I wondered if Opal would wash her hands before slipping into bed—and in part because her words made me sad. She'd lost four husbands. No wonder she felt so strongly about her cat. He was truly all she had left.

I could understand the attachment to the cat—at least to some extent. Sasha and Copper had certainly filled a void in my life now that the kids were gone. If only I could get used to having Spike around; that would be something.

A short time later, Warren and I headed off to our room for some alone time. We'd always enjoyed Sunday afternoon naps, but never so much as since that last kiddo was out of the house. Talk about peace and quiet! About an hour after I dozed off, something woke me up.

"Do you hear that?" I asked.

Warren nodded toward the door. "An alarm is going off?"

"Yes. It's coming from Opal's room. I'll go check on her." Slipping out of the bed, I padded down the hallway. Sure enough, I found Opal's door wide open and the alarm clock on the bedside table beeping nonstop. Should I wake her up or let her sleep a while longer?

Didn't take long to decide. I'd let her sleep. We all needed the rest.

I took a couple of steps inside the room and had just reached to turn off the alarm clock when I noticed the open laptop on Opal's lap and her fingers still perched on the keys.

I smiled. I'd fallen asleep in that very position several times over the years, usually in the middle of an edit for a client.

I gently pried her fingers loose from the computer, doing my best not to wake her. Poor thing. She was snoring. I gazed at her wrinkled face. Lying here, sound asleep, she looked so peaceful, so innocent. The words to Pastor Miller's sermon replayed in my mind. Could I see this thing through, from start to finish? Did I have it in me to be a true helper to Opal Lovelace?

Once I managed to get the laptop in hand, I started to close it. I must've brushed the touchpad, because the screen lit up. At once I realized what I was looking at. Opal had been checking her bank balance. Yikes. Over a hundred and fifty thousand dollars? In a savings account? If Opal had that kind of money, why did I need to buy the lace curtains and groceries? And why couldn't she just shop for new clothes on her own dime?

Hmm. Maybe she was trying to hide the money. But why?

My heart twisted within me as I closed the laptop and put it on the bedside table. I needed to talk to Warren about this. . .and quick. If he knew she had that kind of money, he'd likely put her up in a hotel someplace, ousting her from the Peterson Inn. Either that, or he'd start charging her rent.

I returned to my bedroom to find him fast asleep. Unfortunately, I was now wide-awake. Well, no better time to send an e-mail to O'Henry, voicing my latest suspicions and asking about the security cameras at the cell phone company.

Entering my office, I flipped on the light and headed to my computer. Sasha followed along on my heels, begging for attention. I took a seat, and she sprang up into my lap. Nothing new there. I'd grown accustomed to typing with a dachshund in my lap. Copper curled up at my feet, and Spike began to chew on one of the computer cables. I promptly scolded him and diverted his attention to a dog toy.

It'd been days since I'd checked my e-mail, and I found a couple of notes from editing clients that needed a quick response. After taking care of those, I skimmed a few of those goofy forwards that Sheila always sent. One in particular really made me smile. Finally, I hit on an e-mail that caught me off guard. I had to look twice at the address.

Yep. Teresa Klein.

I opened it, surprised to see that it was sent just after church.

> *Annie,*
>
> *I hope you won't find this e-mail inappropriate. I can see that you are trying valiantly to make a difference in Opal Lovelace's life, and I find that admirable. Seeing her in church this morning gave me hope that she might one day change. But let me warn you, she is far more interested in changing others than changing herself. I'm telling you this because I would hate to see her come between you and Warren.*

I paused at that part, realizing she already had, at least to some extent.

> *Something about Opal bothers me, Annie.*

The note continued.

I can't put my finger on it, exactly. Am I the only person in town who thinks she had something to do with the fire at her place? And at yours?

Just watch your back, Annie. That's all I've got to say.

I closed the e-mail and leaned back in my chair, perplexed. Why would Teresa Klein go to such pains to raise suspicions about Opal? And what was all of that "watch your back, Annie," stuff? A warning to be cautious of Opal. . .or some sort of vague threat from Teresa Klein?

I closed my eyes, ready for some one-on-one time with my Daddy God.

Lord, I've been praying for patience. Maybe that's the wrong prayer. What I need is discernment. Show me which rock to look under, Father. Reveal the hidden things. And Lord, while You're at it, could You throw in a little extra grace? This whole "living with Opal" thing is a lot tougher than I thought it would be. I want to be a Good Samaritan, but I need to know this is the right move for our family. Especially Warren. . .

I sighed. Warren had definitely shown godly grace throughout this ordeal, hadn't he? Perhaps too much. He was the one with the generous heart. Otherwise, he would've tossed Opal out on her ear by now.

Lord, thank You for the gift of my husband. May I never take him for granted.

For some reason, thinking of Warren got me to thinking about the dogs. Thinking about the dogs got me to thinking about Don Quixote. Thinking about Don Quixote got me to thinking about that mouse on my front porch. And thinking about that mouse reminded me of how Opal had picked him up and carried him by the tail. . .without even flinching.

Hmm. Maybe that "grab the varmint by the tail" approach was best, particularly when it came to an ornery old woman who'd lied about her financial status. Yes, from this point on, the kid gloves were off. Opal might be staying in my house, but I wasn't going to baby her any longer. Nope, from now on, I'd carry that varmint by the tail.

CHAPTER ⚑⚑⚑ FOURTEEN

SMOKE GETS IN YOUR EYES

Opal awoke from her nap in a sour mood. I could hear her opening and closing doors in the kitchen for some time before she finally entered my office, her face knotted in a scowl. With her arms crossed, she made an announcement. "We're out of creamer."

"Oh?" I looked up from the manuscript I was editing to face her. Seemed strange that we'd be out so quickly. I'd just purchased some a couple of days before. All I could manage was a flimsy, "I'm sorry."

"I can't very well drink my coffee without creamer," she complained. "And who was messing with my laptop?"

"What?"

"Someone moved my laptop."

"Ah. You were asleep. I just thought I should. . ."

"I would appreciate it if you wouldn't touch my things, Annie. Whether I'm sleeping or awake."

In that moment, I remembered my new "grab the varmint by the tail" approach. I needed to be firm. *Lord, can I be firm and still be a Good Samaritan?*

"Opal," I said, mustering up every bit of strength within me, "I was trying to do you a favor by keeping your laptop from falling. And if you want creamer, the grocery store is open. Feel free to go and get whatever you like. I've already done my shopping for the week."

There. That should do it.

She stared at me as if she didn't quite believe what I'd just said.

Don't bend, Annie. If you give her an inch, she'll take a mile.

"Fine." She released an exaggerated breath. "Just hope my rheumatiz can handle walking all that way."

Please. You walk three miles every morning. "Why not take your car?"

She pursed her lips. "My keys have gone missing, remember?" An accusing look came into her eyes.

"I remember hearing you say something about that. But I assure you, I haven't touched them." She stood in silence for a few seconds, and I finally shrugged, determined to stick to my newer, tougher philosophy. "If you can't find your keys, why not walk? The weather is beautiful today."

"Humph." She reached for the cat's leash, and within minutes they were gone.

I leaned back against my chair, trembling. There. That wasn't so hard. . .was it? I did my best to go back to my manuscript but found myself distracted. *I sure hope she's okay. It's quite a walk to the store. Should I have offered to drive her?*

No. The voice that whispered the word to my heart was pretty clear. *No, Annie.*

After wrapping up the edit for my client, I headed to the kitchen to fix a glass of tea. As I reached into the freezer to snag some ice cubes, something caught my eye. There. . . behind the frozen pot roast.

"What is that?"

I reached back and grabbed the big blue bottle, pulling it out.

The creamer.

"What in the world?" Why had she put it in the freezer when it belonged in the fridge below?

Hmm. To hide it from me, no doubt. But why? What would prompt her to do such a thing and then insist it was gone?

She's messing with my mind. That's what she's doing. She's testing me to see if I'll buy the creamer, all the while acting like she has no money in the bank. This is some kind of a test, a psychological twister, meant to confuse me.

As I pondered these things, my house phone rang. I didn't recognize the number but answered anyway. The voice on the other end surprised me.

"Annie? This is Teresa Klein."

"Oh, hey girl. I just read your e-mail. I guess we need to talk, huh?"

"Yes. . ." She hesitated. "I'm hoping you're not upset about what I wrote. It was difficult to say. But I'm actually not calling about that. I'm at work right now."

"Oh, I see." I could hear the steady hum of voices in the background.

"I wanted to let you know that Opal's at the store, and one of our customers just saw her put a can of cat food in her pocket."

"No way. Now she's stealing?"

"I'm afraid so. And speaking of the cat, she tied him to the light post out front while she's shopping. We've had a couple of customers complain that he hissed at them when they walked by. Our manager was going to call you, but I told him I'd call. I know she's not really your responsibility, but. . ."

"Say no more. I'll be right there."

I snuck into our bedroom long enough to slip into presentable clothes and tell Warren where I was going and why. When I informed him that Opal had been caught shoplifting, he groaned and put the pillow over his head. Couldn't say I blamed him. Oh how I wished I could climb back in bed and start the afternoon over! But, alas, I could not. Opal awaited.

I arrived at the grocery store in record time. I found my elderly houseguest gabbing with the manager as if they were old friends. She saw me and waved.

"Oh Annie, I'm so glad you're here. The funniest thing happened!"

"Really?" I drew near, and she slipped her arm through mine in an uncharacteristically friendly way.

"It's the silliest thing. I was shopping, putting everything in my basket, as always. But somehow I must've gotten confused." She giggled. "I put Don Quixote's cat food in my pocket, thinking it was my keys. Isn't that silly?"

Hysterical. I looked into the eyes of Philip Maddox, the store manager.

"I'm sure it was an oversight," he said with a shrug. "She was probably distracted."

Or trying to pull one over on you.

Opal giggled. "I've paid for it now, of course, but would feel better if you would tell Mr. Maddox that I'm a law-abiding citizen." Her eyes sparkled with mischief, as if this whole thing were nothing more than a silly game.

I drew a deep breath then spouted, "She's a law-abiding citizen." *When she's not burning down buildings, lying about her financial status, and shoplifting.* I forced a smile.

He nodded and with the wave of a hand sent us on our way. As I drove Opal and Don Quixote home, she chatted all the way, acting as if we were the best of friends. However, the minute we walked into the house, the cat went into another of his hissing fits, this time aiming his angst at Spike, who took it as a let-the-games-begin sign.

At once, the two began to spit and sputter. Opal tried to get in the middle of it but ended up with a scratch on her arm. In the very midst of the battle, my cell phone rang. Hearing Brandi's voice was the only bright spot in a thus-far dreary day.

"How's it going over there?" she started.

I wanted to tell her—every last detail. However, the lump in my throat prevented me from responding.

"Mm-hmm. I suspected as much." She sighed. "I can only imagine. And now I'm about to add insult to injury."

"What do you mean?" I managed. "Has something happened to Maddy? Is she sick again?"

"No, nothing like that." Brandi paused. "Mom, I have to ask a huge favor."

"What, honey?"

"Can you watch Maddy for me?"

I breathed a sigh of relief. "Oh sure. Is that all? Bring her over and let Nana have her for a while. You needing a break or something?"

"No, I don't mean watch her today. Scott and I have to

make a quick trip to New York."

"New York? Why?" She hesitated just long enough for my antennae to rise. "What is it, Brandi?"

"Maybe nothing. But Scott has an interview with a pharmaceutical company near Cornell. They've been looking at him for a few weeks now, actually. At first he wasn't interested. Didn't want to move away, but now. . ."

"Wait." My heart almost stopped beating. "Are you saying you're moving to New York?"

Brandi's words were rushed, laced with nervous energy. "I've been so worried about telling you about this. And maybe we're getting worked up for nothing. But there's a possibility Bescher's Pharmaceuticals will make him an offer that would more than double his salary. If that happens. . ."

If that happened, I could wave good-bye to seeing my granddaughter grow up. I knew exactly what would happen. They would move off to New York, and I'd never see them again!

"Mom, don't worry, okay? Maybe this won't even work out."

"Is that how you want me to pray?" I asked. "For things *not* to work out?" My heart twisted within me as I pondered this option. Didn't seem fair to Scott. After all, he needed the best possible job. And New York was beautiful, particularly the area around Cornell. Warren and I had visited the various waterfalls on our last vacation. I could see the draw for a young family, especially if the price was right.

Oblivious to my thoughts, Brandi kept going. "Pray for God's perfect will. That's the only thing that makes sense."

"What about the restaurant?" I asked. Brandi managed

Lee Yu's Garden, Clarksborough's only Chinese buffet.

"If Scott gets this job, I won't have to work. I can stay home with Maddy. I love working, but. . ."

"Say no more. I know that dilemma all too well." She wanted to stay home with her daughter, and I couldn't blame her.

"So, it's okay? You don't mind an impromptu visit from your favorite granddaughter?"

"My *only* granddaughter," I reminded her.

"So far," Brandi added with a chuckle. "If I quit my job and move off to no-man's-land, I'll have a lot of free time on my hands." She giggled. "Might just be God's perfect timing to think about having another."

"Maybe." *But I won't be with you to help with the new baby, if you're moving all the way up there!*

"I know Maddy's a real handful, so I hate to ask you to watch her. Just don't know what else to do."

"We'll manage."

"Yes, but you really have to keep a close eye on her these days. She's into everything. Remember what happened the last time?"

Did I ever. She'd opened the refrigerator and gotten into my stash of candy bars. Then she'd located a box of Christmas decorations from the hall closet and hung them all over the living room, breaking a couple of my favorites. Afterward, she'd fallen asleep on my bed and rolled off, garnering a huge bump on her forehead and a trip to the emergency clinic for a possible concussion.

"I'll watch her like a hawk. But what about the dog? If she's allergic. . ."

"I've already thought of that. Candy offered to take Spike, but if you decide to let him stay, I'll bring his crate and he can hang out in the bedroom or something. Just keep them separated as much as you can."

"Mm-hmm." Like that was possible. Maddy adored that dog and vice versa. As soon as Spike heard her voice, he'd yap until I let him out of the crate, no doubt. "So, when do you need me to take her?" I asked. "And for how long?"

"Well, actually, the company wants to fly us up there right away. Tomorrow."

"Ah." I thought about all the things I'd planned to do tomorrow for the wedding—double-check the centerpieces for the reception tables, print the programs, contact Maggie down at the florist shop to finalize the order for boutonnières and corsages. How could I factor a fidgety two-year-old into all of that?

"What do you think? I could ask Candy, but you know how she is with kids. She's. . ."

"Say no more." I knew Candy hadn't quite mastered the "I can't give a toddler cream-filled donuts and coffee for breakfast" thing. Yet. Her day would come. "Bring her over. I'll be happy to have her."

"Oh Mom, thank you." I heard the break in Brandi's voice. "I. . .I don't know what I'll do without you if we. . ." Her voice trailed off.

"Let's don't go there yet," I suggested. "We don't know what God's up to."

"I guess that's part of the adventure."

God bless that girl of mine. . .always looking on the bright side.

"Oh, I have to let you go," Brandi said, cutting things short. "You-know-who is in the kitchen. I think I hear her pulling things out of the dishwasher. Thanks, Mom. See you in the morning."

"Love you, babe."

We ended the call, and I turned to find Opal staring at me. "Did I hear that right? Is the sickly child coming to stay?"

"Sickly child?" I turned to her, feeling my anger mounting. How dare she talk about Maddy in such a condescending tone?

"I can't spend time with a child who's ill."

"Well then. . ." I rose to my feet, mustering up the courage to speak the words on my heart: *Maybe it's time for you to find someplace else to stay.*

I'd just started to give my ultimatum when Opal sniffed the air and wrinkled her nose. "What *is* that smell?"

"Smell?" *Hmm.* Come to think of it, I did notice something.

Walking into the living room, I discovered Spike had had an accident on my new white carpeting. Groaning, I headed off to the kitchen for the stain remover. The next few minutes were spent on my knees, scrubbing the carpet. All the while Opal stood behind me, carrying on and on about the diseases carried by dogs and small children and how her delicate constitution couldn't handle anything else.

I know just what you mean. I can't handle anything else, either. Good Samaritan or no Good Samaritan. I've tried, Lord. I've really, truly given this my best. But it looks like my best isn't good enough. So pull me out of the fire, Lord. I'm done.

Opal continued to rant, but I didn't hear a word. At this

point, everything caught up to me. Though I did my best to keep my emotions to myself, I broke like a dam. The tears streamed down my face until I couldn't hide them anymore. Turning back to her, I spouted, "Opal, enough!"

She took one look at my tearstained face, muttered the word, "Oh," and headed off to her room.

I cleaned up the mess, tears flowing. Oh, if only the mess I'd created by bringing Opal Lovelace into my home could be washed away as easily!

CHAPTER ⚎ FIFTEEN

STRIKE A POSE

Monday was spent caring for a toddler, three dogs, a cat, and an eighty-three-year-old woman while wedding planning. Forget editing. I wouldn't get to my clients till after the big day was behind me. And with Maddy in the house, even wedding planning was a challenge. She spent much of the morning pulling Sasha's tail, using Copper for pony rides, and sneaking into the bedroom to tease Spike inside his crate. I spent much of the morning following along behind her, trying to restore peace and order.

On top of all that, Maddy appeared to be doubly allergic to Don Quixote. Every time he came in the room, she went into a sneezing fit. Poor little thing had the reddest nose in town.

On Monday night, several of the ladies from the church met to throw Louise an impromptu lingerie shower. Opal opted to stay home, claiming she had a headache. No doubt. With all the chaos of the past few days, she'd certainly earned one. At least hers would pass. I had a feeling mine was here to stay. I'd already fed and bathed Maddy, and Warren agreed to stay with her, keeping her well out of reach of the cat. I knew how much he loved reading to her and watching

Disney movies, so I didn't even blink. When the man said I was free to go, I ran.

I drove to the church in a prayerful state, acknowledging my frustration to the Lord. It had somehow burned a hole in my very soul, scarring me from the inside out. If I didn't drive out this root of bitterness, I'd never last another day with Opal, let alone several weeks. Once again, I committed to sticking with this—if that's what the Lord had for me. I couldn't help but think He had something up His sleeve here, but what?

I arrived at the church to find the parking lot filled. Great turnout for a bridal shower. I made my way to the fellowship hall, where I found the party in full swing. Thank goodness for Sheila and Evelyn, who'd come up with the decorations and food in such a hurry. I'd have to thank them later. For now, I just wanted to kick back and enjoy the night. For a change.

I smiled at the lovely wedding décor. I'd never seen so many bells. Even the cake was bell-shaped. And the food! Janetta had outdone herself with the darling little sandwiches and varieties of salad. She was certainly in her element. I paused to congratulate her for making it onto the Food and Family Channel's Super Chef competition, and she beamed with delight.

"I'm so shocked, Annie," she said. "And a little scared. I don't know how I'll do on camera. Richard says I'll be fine, but I'm not so sure."

"You'll be more than fine. The viewers are going to love you."

"Thanks." She grinned. "I just keep thinking it will help

me get more clients for the catering business. Wouldn't that be fun?"

"Well, you're doing a great job with all the weddings and parties you've catered thus far." As I continued to offer a few words of encouragement, she surprised me with her response.

"Everything is so much easier now that Richard is helping me."

Indeed. Very curious. So they were definitely an item, were they? The idea tickled me beyond belief. I wanted to ask for more information but found myself distracted by a bevy of hyper females intent on chatting about shower gifts and the like.

As soon as we all filled our plates with food, the conversation really picked up. I was so happy to be among people again—people I didn't have to keep an eye on, anyway—that I found myself getting a little emotional on occasion. *What's up with that?*

I was thankful when the time came to open gifts. I'd outdone myself picking out a present for Louise. I'd found a beautiful white nightgown and matching robe, both made from a soft, silky material. As Louise opened my gift, she gasped. "Oh Annie, it's beautiful. I've never had anything so lovely in all my life."

I beamed with joy. If anyone deserved special things, Louise did. She'd waited over fifty years for Mr. Right, after all. And I could only imagine how pretty she would look in that gown ensemble. Surely Nick's eyes would pop.

"Just be careful, honey," Sheila quipped. "On my wedding night I wore a silk nightgown and almost ended up with a broken shoulder."

Every eye in the place turned Sheila's way, waiting for an explanation.

"It was the combination of silk sheets and silk nightie," she explained with a twinkle in her eye. "Somewhere along the way, I lost my grip. Slid right off the bed and ended up on the floor."

The room erupted in laughter, and Sheila—who never got embarrassed—turned twelve shades of red.

"That was my introduction to married life," she said with a grin. "Orin never forgot it either. And by the way, my shoulder recovered." She giggled. "The only bruise that lasted was the one on my ego."

Evelyn handed Louise another gift and muttered, "Moving on. . ."

I watched as Louise opened a box with a lovely soft pink gown inside. She smiled as she looked at it, but her smile seemed a little forced. In fact, her eyes grew misty as she folded the gown back up and put it back in the box.

"Never mind me," Louise said as she dabbed at her eyes. "I'm so emotional this week."

"Completely understandable." Evelyn reached over and patted her hand. "But we're here for you, Louise. Just let us know if there's anything we can do to help you through the ups and downs."

Louise nodded and thanked Evelyn, but I had a sneaking suspicion things weren't what they appeared. Were problems heating up between Louise and Elio Petracca? What had he done to put such a somber look on her face? She was the bride, for heaven's sake! No bride should look this depressed during her wedding week!

There were several more gifts to open, and this served as the perfect distraction. Before long, Louise's countenance changed, and she was the old Louise once again—excited and happy to be entering a new phase of her life. Soon all the packages were open, except one. I knew it had to be from Sheila. The hot pink paper and lime green bow were a dead giveaway.

"Just wait till she sees this," Sheila whispered in my ear as she settled into the chair next to mine.

After pulling off the flamboyant wrapping, Louise held up a skimpy little blue number that appeared to be see-through.

"It's. . .lovely, Sheila." Louise turned several shades of red as she examined the teensy-tiny nightie. "What there is of it, I mean."

"Just what the doctor ordered," Sheila said with a girlish giggle. She gestured to the bag, her eyes ablaze with mischief. "And there's more. Keep looking."

"Oh, okay." Louise lifted up a tiny blue thing that looked more like a slingshot than an undergarment. "But I'm not sure what it is."

"They're panties."

"Oh, okay." Louise's eyes widened. She examined them from several angles. "I, um, I guess I'll figure it out."

This caused a ripple of laughter across the room. Now several of the women had red faces. And a few couldn't stop howling long enough to catch their breath. This was just what I needed to get Opal and her shenanigans off my mind. Good, old-fashioned girl fun.

As the party continued on, I happened to notice Teresa Klein on the other side of the room. She looked uncomfortable in this setting, but why? Perhaps situations such as these were tougher on single women. Determined to lift her spirits, I snuck over to take the seat next to her.

"How you doing, Teresa?"

"Okay."

"You look a little. . .distracted. Everything okay?" I nudged her with my elbow. "Is all this talk about romance making you think about that handsome Elio Petracca?"

"Well, I've been doing my fair share of that, too." For a moment, she smiled. Then, just as quickly, her lips curled downward. "But, Annie, I've been dying to talk to you about something else. . .something a little, well, difficult."

"Oh, right. That e-mail you sent. You want to talk about Opal?" I whispered.

"No. Not this time." Her gaze shifted to the floor, and she lowered her voice. "Something else. Or rather, *someone* else."

"Let's find someplace to talk, then."

We shifted to the kitchen. Here, the noise of the crowd was more manageable. I gazed across the center island at Teresa, concerned by the look in her eye.

"Tell me, Teresa. You've got me worried."

"I'm afraid I'm going to worry you more," she said. "It's about that new deputy, Molly O'Shea."

"Oh." Not at all what I'd expected her to say. "What about her?"

Teresa's gaze shifted down to the tablecloth. She took her finger and began to trace one of the flowers on it. "Well, before I tell you, I guess you need to know something about me."

"Okay." I shrugged. "Tell me whatever you're comfortable

sharing. And I promise it won't go any further than me."

The chatter of a couple of women filled the air, distracting me. I looked up to see Janetta and Evelyn entering the kitchen with dirty dishes in hand. They took one look at us and must've figured out we were in the middle of a private conversation. Janetta whispered a quiet "sorry" and set her dishes in the sink. Evelyn followed suit. I'd have to thank them later. Turning my attention back to Teresa, I said, "Go ahead, honey."

She sighed. "I don't know why I worry so much about what people think about me, but I do." After a pause, she looked me in the eye. "Annie, I'm starting to wonder if there's a guy out there for me. Sometimes I think I'll be single forever."

I offered what I hoped would be perceived as a sympathetic smile, trying to figure out what this had to do with Molly.

"I've been to several dating services," Teresa continued, "always hoping against hope I'd find the perfect man. Obviously it hasn't happened yet, and I've got to say those dating services aren't all they're cracked up to be. Some of the folks on there are, well, a little desperate. And some have been around the block a few times."

"What do you mean?"

"Well, let's just say I've seen the profiles for nearly every single person within four states. After a while, you kind of get to know the other singles out there. We're like a community. And there's one face that just keeps popping up, no matter which service I join."

"Oh?"

"Yes."

Teresa opened an envelope and pulled out a profile of a young woman with a photo that looked eerily familiar. I grabbed it and looked at every detail of the woman's face. Same red hair. Same freckles. Same quirky smile. Looking up at Teresa, I asked the obvious. "Where did you get this picture of Molly?"

"Read the profile, Annie," she whispered. "I printed up a page from a Christian dating service. Look at the name she's using."

I took a close look, all right. "Brenna Ratcliff?" No way. I squinted as I looked at the photo once again. "This is Molly. No doubt about it."

"I know." Teresa sighed. "And I've been hanging on to this for several days, trying to decide what to do with it. How could the sheriff's office have hired her without discovering this?"

"Maybe it's just a name she uses for dating services. . .to protect herself," I offered. "I'm sure it's no big deal. A lot of single women probably do it so people can't track them." Even as I spoke the words, I whispered a prayer, hoping I was right. It would be troubling to find out Molly was leading a double life.

Was she leading a double life?

"Do you mind if I keep this?" I held up the photo.

Teresa shrugged. "Go ahead. I don't mind a bit. Take it to O'Henry, if you like. He's probably going to have a lot of questions. And if you need any information about the online dating service, just ask. I can get you connected."

"Now that would be something." I laughed. "A married woman checking things out on a dating service." Right away, my own words came back around and stared me in the face. Maybe Molly O'Shea—or Brenna Ratcliff—was really married in her other life. A shiver crawled up my spine. It would devastate Devin to know the woman he'd fallen for had a husband and kids.

Don't get ahead of yourself, Annie. You don't even know for sure this is Molly. I picked up the photo and gazed at it once again. *Yep, it's Molly.*

I felt like I held a ticking time bomb in my hand. Determined not to overreact, I shoved the photo back in the envelope and looked up at Teresa with a smile. "Thank you for giving me this. I'm just going to pray it's nothing."

"Me, too," she whispered.

As I rejoined the party, I pondered a great many things. If Molly O'Shea wasn't Molly O'Shea, who was she? Was the name Brenna Ratcliff a ruse or her real name? Was she really someone else altogether? And why had she—whoever she was—shown up in Clarksborough about the same time the dating service burned to the ground? Coincidence . . .or more?

I did my best to join in the fray but couldn't stay focused. So many things now bothered me. Teresa's e-mail had raised red flags regarding Opal, and now her conversation raised another red flag. . .about Molly. And while she seemed to have pure motives, I really had to wonder about Teresa. What was with all the finger-pointing? Was she doing this to somehow distract me?

I had no idea who'd burned Opal Lovelace's building to the ground, but my suspect list was certainly growing. Had Opal done it to receive an insurance payment? Had

Molly—er, Brenna Ratcliff—come to Clarksborough to set that fire? Perhaps Chris Brewster was somehow involved. He'd sure been using Opal's losses as his gains. And what about Teresa? Was the unhappy single woman capable of burning down The Perfect Match. . .just because Opal hadn't located the perfect man for her yet?

Yep. I certainly had my choice of options. And right now, with my brain completely on overload, none of them made a lick of sense. Why, oh why couldn't I just spend an evening with my friends and forget about all this?

As the party ended, I helped Louise load up a trunk full of presents, stopping to give her a warm embrace. "Less than a week till Saturday!" I exclaimed.

"Mm-hmm." She yawned, and I couldn't help but smile. "Having trouble sleeping?"

"I sure am." Her downcast expression made it clear her lack of sleep had nothing to do with anticipation of the big day. Still, I decided not to press her on the issue. Maybe she just had prewedding jitters. Lots of brides did.

After saying our good-byes, I headed to my car. Teresa had parked next to me. I paused to thank her for the information about Molly, though it still puzzled me. When Teresa swung open the front door of her SUV, the overpowering smell of gasoline accosted me.

I fanned myself with my hand. "Oh girl. Tell me you're not driving around with a gas can in your car."

"Well, it's a dilemma," she said with a shrug. "I ran out of gas a couple weeks ago on the turnpike. And an SUV's not like a regular car with a trunk. Where else am I going to put the gas can, if not in the back?"

"But those fumes." I pinched my nose. "They can't be good for you."

"Yeah. I should probably take it out. But as sure as I do, I'll run out of gas again."

"I hear ya." I'd run out of gas a couple of times myself, so I knew the dilemma well. Still, I'd never think of carrying around a can of gas in an open vehicle, regardless.

It wasn't till I pulled away in my car that I was struck with a horrible thought. Gasoline. Teresa is carrying a can of *gasoline* in her car. Teresa, who's mad at Opal for not locating her perfect match. . .is carrying gasoline.

CHAPTER ⚏ SIXTEEN

KISS OF FIRE

I've always agreed with the old adage that it helps to have friends in high places. On Tuesday morning, I received a call from Adam Collins, Devin's best friend, who happened to manage the cell phone company across the street from Opal's place.

"Mrs. Peterson, Devin said you wanted to talk to me."

"Yes." I explained my interest in the security video from the morning of the fire.

Adam hesitated a moment. "Hmm. I'm not sure our cameras would pick up anything from Opal's place, but I'll be happy to let you come, and we can take a look. If we notice anything odd, we'll hand the information over to the sheriff's office. Agreed?"

"Agreed. Would you mind if Warren came? I'd feel better having him with me, regardless of what we find. I think he's got time before having to be at work."

"Sounds great. See you in a few minutes."

"Oh, just one more thing." I looked down at Maddy, who sat on the floor playing with her stuffed animals. "We're going to have a toddler with us."

"Yeah, I heard you were watching Maddy," he said. "Do

you think Brandi and Scott will really move away?"

Man, news travels fast in this town.

"I don't know," I said. "Don't even want to think about that yet. Just wanted you to know that I'm bringing a toddler. If you have anything in your office of value, hide it or tie it down."

"Will do." He laughed. "I'm trying to picture you over there with so many people and animals in your house. Devin told me he's glad he moved out."

"No doubt. I'd move, too, if I could." We shared a hearty laugh together, and then I ended the call. Time to check on Warren and to let Opal know we'd be gone for a while.

When I stuck my head in Opal's room to give her the news, she responded with a grumpy, "Just take that kid with you. I caught her pulling on Don Q's tail again last night."

I bit my tongue and nodded. "Of course. I wouldn't dream of leaving her here." *Ever. In a thousand years.*

Warren and I entered the cell phone store at ten till eight. Adam greeted us with a smile. "I found the footage from the morning of the fire. Took some doing, but I've got it, and it does capture some of Opal's place."

After leading us to his office in the back of the building, Adam turned the television to face us and pushed a few buttons on the machine to get it rolling. "This is the footage taken the morning of the fire." He pointed at the right side of the screen. "You can see here that we've got a blurry image of the side of Opal's place. And if you look closely here. . ." He paused the image. "You can almost see the back of her place. Almost."

"Right." Didn't see anything suspicious, though.

"Keep watching for just a minute." He let the footage roll. Finally, off in the distance, a fuzzy image of a car appeared, driving down the side street. It paused at the curb near the back of Opal's business.

"Can you stop it right there?" I asked.

Adam paused it long enough for me to take in the vehicle. White. Small sedan. Moon roof. I couldn't get a clear picture of the license plate and didn't recognize the car.

"Doesn't look familiar," Warren observed. "Sure don't think it's anyone we know."

Maddy squirmed out of my lap and walked over to Adam's desk. She climbed up in his chair and began to open the drawers. "Maddy, don't—" I started.

"Nah, she's okay," Adam said with a shrug. "There's nothing she can hurt in there."

He started rolling the footage again. "Watch this." The front door opened on the driver's side, and someone stepped out.

I gasped, recognizing the long hair at once. "Molly?" I whispered. "Molly O'Shea?"

"Yes." Adam froze the image once more then turned to me with a sigh. "If you watch the rest, you'll see her disappear around the back of Opal's building then return to her car and drive away in a hurry. It's weird."

"The back of the shop?" I reiterated. "Isn't that where they found gasoline?"

"Yes. But Annie, she's not carrying a gas can," Warren said.

Adam started the machine again, and I watched, now breathless. Had I somehow paired up my son with a pyro-maniac? I watched, more closely this time. Molly—or would it be Brenna?—stood a moment, looking around, as if hoping not to be caught. Or was I just imagining that? She seemed to flinch a little as a green vehicle eased its way by. Then she rounded the back of the building, only to return less than a minute later. As I watched her get inside and drive away, I turned to Warren. "Very odd. What do you think?"

"I think Molly went to Opal's back door on the morning of the fire." He shrugged. "That's about it."

"Exactly." I sighed. "She did look a little nervous, but that doesn't incriminate her in any way. It's certainly not the kind of evidence I was hoping for."

I glanced over at Maddy, who now sat atop Adam's desk, drawing on a piece of paper. She was all giggles and smiles, so I left her to her own devices, hoping she would continue to play quietly.

Adam turned off the machine and faced us. "Look Mr. and Mrs. P., I've known Devin since we were in the second grade."

"Right." I nodded.

Adam shook his head. "I'm not saying I don't like this Molly chick. I'm just saying she seems a little, I don't know. . .jumpy? My girlfriend and I double-dated with Devin and Molly last night. He's fallen hard and fast. But when I tried to talk to Molly, she deliberately avoided some of my questions."

"Questions?"

"Yes, like 'Where are you from?' and 'What's your family like?' Stuff like that." Adam shrugged. "Maybe I'm just overly suspicious, but I get the weirdest feeling she's hiding something."

"Could be." I was more than a little worried about what

my son's new love interest might have up her sleeve. Arson, perhaps?

"Or maybe. . ." Warren, ever the bastion of common sense, interjected. "Maybe she's just a new kid in town and reluctant to show all her cards. She's a cop. Cops are naturally hesitant to trust people. And they don't always open up and tell all like most women do."

"Most women tell all?" I crossed my arms and stared at my husband, perplexed. "You really believe that?"

He put his hands up in the air in mock defeat. "Annie, c'mon. You know what I mean."

"I think he means I talk too much." I groaned then turned back to Adam. "So, what do you gentlemen think? Is this something we should show to O'Henry, or should I walk away and forget we ever had this discussion?"

Warren surprised me with his answer. "Wouldn't hurt to show it to him."

Adam nodded. "I was thinking the same thing. Might not amount to anything, but my conscience would be cleared if, by some chance, she happened to be the one who. . ." He didn't finish. We all knew what he meant.

"Thanks for checking into this, Adam." Warren extended his hand and offered a smile. "And don't be such a stranger. Seems like we hardly ever see you around our place anymore."

"Well, now that Devin's living in town, we usually hang out over there and play video games. Besides, we all have jobs now. It's not like it was in high school when we had time on our hands."

"Just know you're always welcome. We could use a little . . .testosterone around our place," Warren said then slugged Adam in the arm. "If you catch my drift."

"Yeah, I've been hearing all about Opal's escapades from Devin." Adam chuckled. "I can only imagine what that's like. You should've seen what a crazy neighbor she was."

"What do you mean?" I asked.

Adam laughed. "Well, where do I start? She just did the most bizarre things. One day she'd come in our store and complain that our customers were taking up too many parking spots out on the street. Then, other times, she'd come inside dressed in her nightgown, carrying a plateful of cookies she'd baked for us. And I can't tell you how many times she came in to buy a new cell phone. Every three or four months she was back to upgrade to a new one. And I'm talking about the really expensive ones."

At once, my mind flashed back to Opal's bank balance. No doubt she could afford new phones. For heaven's sake, she could've just purchased the cell phone company.

"Did she know how to use the phones?" Warren asked.

"Ya got me," Adam said. "Of course, we always took the time to show her, but who knows if she really understood anything to do with technology. I always suspected she kept trading them in, hoping she'd eventually get one she could figure out. But I felt bad selling them to her."

"Strange. And stranger still that she has no cell phone at our house, at least none that I've seen." I looked at Warren, and he shook his head.

"I guess they were all lost in the fire." Adam shrugged. "And maybe I'm saying too much, I don't know. She's just weird. And that cat! I've never met a meaner animal. Won't do a thing he's told, and yet she somehow gets him to walk with a leash. Doesn't make a bit of sense to me."

"Yep. That's Don Quixote," I agreed. "You should see what he's done to my sofa. Scratched up the fabric. And he hasn't taken kindly to the dogs."

"It's Opal's fault," he said. "She babies him."

I shrugged. "I guess I understand that. She doesn't have any children or grandchildren to baby. He's all she's got."

"Still, she's as nutty as they come, and I. . ." Adam shook his head then raked his fingers through his hair.

"You what?" I asked.

"I wouldn't be a bit surprised to hear she burned that place down herself. She's a looney tune." Immediately he stopped himself. "Sorry, that was a little strong. But I'm not kidding when I say she's irrational enough to burn down her own home."

"I think we can all agree she's. . .different." Warren stood and looked at his watch. "But that doesn't make her an arsonist. We have no proof of anything like that, so I hate to even speculate."

"True." I sighed. "This is a tricky one. We don't have a lot of physical evidence. Just the charred remains of an old building that probably should've been torn down twenty years ago anyway."

Warren looked at his watch again and then rose to his feet. "I hate to cut this short, but I've really got to get to work. Annie, are you ready?"

"Sure."

I turned to reach for Maddy but found her missing. Thankfully, I heard a giggle from underneath the desk. I came around the back of the desk, glancing down to fetch her. At once, I saw what she'd been scribbling on.

"Um, Adam?" I held it up for him to see.

"Oh yikes." His eyes widened. "I completely forgot about that. It's my paycheck. . .from corporate."

"I'm so sorry." Groaning, I picked up the toddler and scolded her. "You messed up Uncle Adam's check!"

"Unca Adam!" she echoed then let out a squeal.

"Is there anything I can do to tide you over till you get the check replaced?" Warren asked.

"Nah. They should be able to cut me another one and drop it in the mail. I'll manage." Adam shrugged. "It's my fault, anyway. You told me to hide anything of value, Mrs. P., and I forgot."

He was right, but that sure didn't make me feel any better.

Warren and I made our way back through the now-busy store. As we climbed into the car, he turned to me with concern in his eyes.

"What?" I asked.

"Annie, if there's even the slimmest chance that Opal burned down her place, we've got to watch her like a hawk."

"I know." After a pause, I added, "But she's not the only one I'm suspicious of, Warren. This whole thing about Molly really has me worked up."

"Why?" Warren turned the key in the ignition and put the car into reverse. "She just got out of her car for a minute."

"Long enough to empty gasoline on the back of the house."

"But she had no can."

"Not in her hands. Not in her car. But maybe she had it stashed someplace out back. It's possible."

Warren backed the car out of the parking lot, his lips now pursed. Finally, he glanced my way. "Annie, I know you're concerned. But you can't turn everyone into a suspect, especially not your son's new girlfriend. Give her a chance before you incriminate her."

I exhaled loudly. "But Warren, there's more." I filled him in, giving him the whole Brenna Ratcliff story. By the time I reached the end, Warren was ready to call Devin on the phone to warn him. I managed to keep him from doing that.

"I don't want to ruin this for him. What if she's just an innocent girl who happened to come into town at the wrong time?"

"Point well taken."

"I'm just so confused," I admitted as Warren pulled our car up in front of the bank. "The day Molly came with O'Henry to investigate the fire in our bedroom, Opal looked at her as if she'd never seen her before. But Molly. . ." I shook my head. "There was something in her expression that raised questions in my mind."

"What kind of questions?"

"I don't know." Leaning back in my seat, I thought about that. I really didn't have any reason to suspect Molly of anything, did I? So what if she gave Opal a strange look that day in my living room? And so what if she used a pseudonym to register for dating services? What did it really matter that she'd stopped off at The Perfect Match on the morning of the fire? Those things didn't amount to arson.

Did they?

CHAPTER SEVENTEEN

WE DIDN'T START THE FIRE

I spent Tuesday afternoon working on centerpieces for the wedding. Opal, in a strange burst of kindness, not only offered to help but prattled about in the kitchen, making French toast and coffee for the two of us. I'd never seen her in such a chipper mood. And talk about easy to get along with! Perhaps it had something to do with the fact that "that child" was taking a nap behind closed doors.

"How was the shower last night, Annie?" she asked as she took a seat opposite me.

I looked up from my work with a shrug. "Oh, just your typical room full of women looking at lingerie and talking about silly things."

"Like the honeymoon night?" She quirked a brow then laughed as I stared at her in stunned silence. "Oh don't look so shocked, Annie. I've been married four times, remember? I've been through the wedding night jitters time and time again." She giggled. "And who knows. . .maybe I'll go through them again."

I blushed at that one, doing my best to stay focused on the silk flowers in my hand. I'd never thought about it before, but Opal had certainly been through more than a few adventures in her life.

"My first husband was the love of my life." She sighed. "I was only seventeen when we got married, but I was the happiest girl on the planet. We didn't really have honeymoons back then, not like kids today. But my aunt had a little summer cottage near the river, and she let us stay there for a few nights." Opal blushed, and I giggled a little.

"Care to elaborate?"

"Well, let's just say I learned a lot." She shook her head and sighed. "I'm telling you, that Charlie Lovelace was the only man I ever really loved."

"So much so that you've kept his name?" I asked.

"Yes. Well, after my last husband died, I went back to Lovelace. It was the only thing that made sense to me."

"What happened to Charlie?" I asked gently. "How did he. . .well. . .?"

She shook her head and tears rose to cover her lashes. "Happened forty years ago, and I still remember it like it was yesterday." A lone tear rolled down her cheek as she shared the story with a shaky voice. "I was at home making dinner, as always. Charlie loved my meat loaf and mashed potatoes, and that's what I was cooking that night. Anyway, he was always home by six. Never a minute late. But that night six came and went."

A chill wrapped itself around me as I watched her countenance change. Her eyes brimmed over and her voice began to shake.

"I had no way to reach him. I didn't know what else to do, so I just started to pray." Opal began to weep. Instead of approaching her, I gave her the space I thought she needed.

After a moment, she spoke through the tears. "At ten minutes after eight. . .an officer knocked. . .on my door. I knew the moment I saw him what had happened. . .but hearing the words. . ." Opal dissolved in another pool of tears.

I rushed to her side and wrapped her in my arms. "Oh Opal, I'm so sorry."

She allowed herself to grieve in my arms, a first in our relationship. Surely the Lord was up to something here.

"You know, I happen to know Someone who promises to heal broken hearts, Opal. If you'll just turn to Him."

"I've heard all the God-talk, Annie," she said, her expression hardening. "And I don't need any more."

"What do you mean?"

"Well, let's just say God and I haven't been on speaking terms since that night."

"Oh honey, you can't blame the Lord for what happened. We live in a fallen world. Bad things happen to good people all the time."

"Exactly. But that doesn't make it right." Opal crossed her arms, a defiant look on her face. "And as for blaming God, He could've stopped it. He could have stopped that truck driver from drinking, and He could've stopped that truck from barreling through the intersection and hitting my Charlie's car. But He didn't. Any God who lets an innocent man die—and a guilty man live—well, that's a not a God I'm interested in serving."

I focused my attention on the topiaries, praying for wisdom. *Lord, what can I tell her? She needs to know that You're good and You love her. But she's got a good point. I can't give her some pat answer. Not when she's been through so much.*

As I pondered these things, my cell phone rang. I rose and crossed the kitchen to fetch my purse. Scrambling for my phone, I almost missed the call. Thankfully, I caught it on the last ring.

"G'afternoon, Agatha Annie!" Sheila's bubbly voice greeted me. "Have we solved the case yet?"

"Well, good afternoon to you, too," I said. "And no, not a lot of progress, though"—I paused to look at Opal—"my question marks are multiplying."

"Got it. You can't talk right now."

"Right." I decided to shift gears. "What did you think of the shower last night?" I asked.

"It was a blast. I had a great time." She giggled. "I love all those nightgowns Louise got. In fact, I loved a couple of them so much that I went and bought them today for myself."

My eyes widened at that news. I'd known Sheila and Orin for years, but never pictured them to be the lingerie type. On the other hand, my best friend did tend to run on the adventurous side.

Sheila kept talking, but I found myself distracted by Opal, who'd reached into a nearby drawer and come up with a lighter. With the flip of a finger, the little flame on the lighter erupted. Opal held it in her hand, gazing at the flickering flame. She didn't say anything—just sat there, staring at the eerie glow.

"Um, Sheila. . ." I tried to keep my voice steady. "I really need to let you go." When Opal turned my way with a curious glance, I added, "Opal and I are in the middle of making centerpieces, and we've still got a lot to do."

"Well, hang up on me then!" Sheila quipped. "Just see if I ever invite you up to our lake house for a weekend retreat."

"Sheila, you don't own a lake house."

"I know, but we're thinking of buying one. Just see if I ever invite you!"

I hung up, and with as casual a shrug as I could muster, turned back to Opal. "It was just Sheila. She wanted to gab, but I'm too busy."

Opal continued to play with the lighter. After a couple of minutes, she said, "You know, my Charlie was a smoker. I know most people these days aren't, but back then smoking was more. . .acceptable."

What are you getting at, Opal?

"Strangest thing," she continued, staring at the lighter in her hand. "I never cared for the smell of cigarette smoke, but I missed it when Charlie was gone. Funny, isn't it?"

"Very." I rose from my chair and reached for the lighter, putting it back in the drawer. "But if you don't mind, I have a ton of things to do and could really use your help. So let's get back to work, okay?"

"Sure." She seemed to snap back to attention, turning to me with a smile. "Have you seen my keys, Annie?"

"Your keys? To the car?" *They've been missing for days. And what does this have to do with your first husband's cigarettes?* "We searched for them already," I reminded her. "Couldn't find them anywhere."

"Oh yes. . ." Her voice trailed off. "So we did." A smile lit her face and she clapped her hands together. "Okay, I can worry about that later. Right now I have to help you make these lovely centerpieces." She pulled her chair up close to mine, and we worked side by side, putting together several beautiful fruit-themed topiaries.

"These will be perfect for the Greek reception," I explained. "All this fruit really makes them pretty, don't you think?"

"Oh my, yes. And I know a great centerpiece when I see it. I've done this four times, remember."

"So, tell me about your weddings," I encouraged her. "And your husbands. I never got to meet any of them. Not a one." No, my memories of Opal were all of her as a single woman.

"Well, as I said, my first was Charlie, the love of my life." After a brief pause to dab her eyes, she continued. "We had a lovely ceremony in my parents' home. Simple but sweet. We were married over twenty years, and I adored him. . .and vice versa. Next came John Morris. He was a Vietnam vet. I met him at a political function about five years after Charlie passed. I think. . ." She shook her head. "Well, in all honesty, I think I felt sorry for him. He was troubled, like so many of the men returning from Vietnam."

"You married him out of pity?"

"I did have feelings for him," she explained. "And I suppose I loved him, to the best of my ability. We had a quiet wedding by a justice of the peace, in his office."

"What happened to John?" I asked, reaching to jab a piece of fake fruit into the topiary.

Her brow wrinkled. "It's so sad, Annie."

I looked up from my work, more curious than ever. "What?"

"John took his life." Her gaze shifted to the floor. "I spent several years trying to fix him, but couldn't. In the end, he did the one thing he'd told me all along he might do. I. . .I never believed him, to be honest. But he was serious."

"Opal, I'm so sorry." I reached to squeeze her hand.

At this point in the conversation, I couldn't help but feel sorry for Opal. She'd been through so much. . .and we still had two husbands to go! I was thankful she was still in a talking mood.

"My next husband, Max, was a really outgoing, funny man." Opal grinned. "I met him at a fund-raiser. He was a comedian. A professional stand-up comedian, I mean. He was a real charmer, that one." Her face lit in a smile. "In fact, he was so charming that he talked me into marrying him right away in a really elaborate ceremony down at the pavilion in the park. He, um, well, he ended up zapping me of most of my savings. Max only worked odd jobs here and there, mostly as an emcee."

If he zapped you of your savings, then where did that hundred and fifty thousand dollars come from? "So, what happened to him?" I asked, startling back to attention. "How did he. . . ?"

"Oh, he's still around."

"What? I thought you outlived all your husbands."

"Nah. I always tell people that because it's easier than explaining that one of them walked out when I stopped funding him. I always figured that marriage outlived its expiration date, so in a sense there was a death, just not a physical one. I will say, that husband killed my joy. Took it when he emptied my pocketbook."

"Ah, I see."

"From what I hear, he's been through three wives since we were married, and I was his third. He's a taker, that one. Not a giver."

"Guess you learned a hard lesson there," I said. "But you must've found love after that, right? I mean, you married again after Max left?"

"Technically, Max didn't leave. I kicked him out. But, yes. I married James Sonnier not too long after that. He was a man I'd met at church. Clarksborough Community Church, no less."

"Oh wow. I think I know some Sonniers."

"Yes, they're still there. His nieces and nephews, I mean. James was a good man, and he took a lot of flack for marrying a woman with a reputation."

"Reputation?" I gave her a curious look.

"Well, back then it wasn't as common for divorced people to remarry, so when James—who was a widow—took an interest in me, the tongues got to wagging from his church-goin' family members." A hint of a smile graced her lips. "But he really loved me, so he followed his heart." She paused a moment. "It wasn't a church wedding, but I didn't really care. As I said, I stopped talking to God back when Charlie died. Just went to church out of formality."

Her words broke my heart, but I didn't comment.

"James was truly one of the most caring men I've ever known." She shook her head and her expression darkened. "He started getting sick just two years after we married. By the time we reached the end of that second summer, I knew something was terribly wrong."

"What was it, honey?" I asked.

"Pancreatic cancer. Very aggressive." She drew in a breath. "If there's any grace at all in the situation, it's that he didn't suffer long. The whole thing happened so fast. But after he died, well, that was it for me. I'd seen enough. . .and done enough."

"So you figured you'd spend the rest of your days pairing other folks up?"

She shrugged. "Yes. My business was already up and running long before I met James or Max. So, I just kept on with it. No one seemed to mind that the matchmaker had enough stories to fill a book. Business was good back then."

"I see."

She paused. "I don't have a clue what's going to happen next." After a moment, she added, "I'm just so happy to have matched up some great couples. Louise and Nick, for example. I still remember the day I decided they would make a nice couple. And Kathy and Chris, of course. They're still my best advertisement."

Or your worst.

I didn't have time to share my opinion on the matter because my cell phone rang. I glanced down at it, half expecting to see Sheila's number once more. Ironically, I didn't recognize this number. I took the call anyway, thinking it might be from a client or something to do with the upcoming wedding.

"Annie, do you have a minute to talk?"

I recognized Kathy Brewster's voice, but it sounded as if she'd been crying.

"Honey, what's wrong?" I continued working on the centerpieces as I prepared myself for her answer.

"I need. . .well, I need a good, strong shoulder," she said. "There's a lot going on over here. Do you mind if I share?"

"Of course I don't mind. What's happening?"

She paused a moment then explained. "Chris and I are. . . are separating."

"What?" I nearly dropped the piece of fruit onto the table.

"We're not divorcing or anything like that," she was quick to add, "but things have been so strained this week. And. . ." She sighed. "To be honest, I just can't take it anymore. I'm so tired of trying to fix this."

"It's not yours to fix," I reminded her. "It's God's."

"I know. And maybe my faith is just low. I don't know." She sighed.

Opal looked my way with a question in her eyes. She mouthed, "Who is that?" but I just shook my head. Right now, Kathy needed me. I didn't try to coax anything out of her. Didn't have to.

"He just doesn't want anything to do with me, Annie. It's as simple as that. I'm not important to him. I could tell you stories. . . ." She paused. "But I won't. At least not today. But you have to trust me when I say that I'm the last thing on his mind, not the first."

"I don't know what to say, except I'm sorry."

"And I'm grateful for that," she said. "You don't know how good it feels to have someone I can talk to about all of this. I think Chris and I need a sabbatical of sorts. Just a week or two. So I'm staying at my mom's place in Quakertown. Maybe if I'm out of the picture, God can do what He needs to do in my husband's life. I don't know."

"I'll be praying, Kathy. I promise."

"I appreciate that." Her voice broke. "I'm counting on it."

As I hung up the phone, Opal looked at me with a

wrinkled brow. "That was Kathy Brewster, wasn't it?"

"Yes."

"Is she. . .are they. . .separating?"

"It's really not my place to say. Just. . ." I wanted to say, "pray for them," but stopped short. After all, Opal had already said that she didn't pray. Besides, Kathy had spoken to me in confidence.

Opal sighed. "I do hope they work things out." She paused and offered a little shrug. "I guess I played up Kathy's positive attributes a little more than I should have to Chris. She just seemed like the perfect woman for him. And I only told Kathy about Chris's good features, too. I left out the fact that he's pretty zealous about his job. I also forgot to mention that his temper tends to flare at times."

"I'm sure they have a lot in common, but the real problem here is the pairing of a believer with a nonbeliever. There's always chaos when that happens." My thoughts shifted to Devin and Molly. I still hadn't settled the issue in my mind— was Molly a Christian or not? I sighed, realizing I didn't have a clear answer just yet. Maybe she was just going to church as a formality, like Opal had done. Or maybe—I shivered— she was putting on an act so she could trap my son. I shook off my ponderings and did my best to focus on Opal, who continued talking.

"I guess I didn't think about that," she said with a shrug. "As I said, God and I haven't exactly been on speaking terms for the past several years, so pairing up folks based on their religious beliefs wouldn't have entered into it."

"That's how most of the world sees it," I agreed, "but it's not what the Bible teaches. Before we can be happily matched with someone, we have to be in a good relationship with the Lord as an individual. If either party in a marriage doesn't have a walking, talking relationship with God, it brings both of them down." In that moment, I made up my mind to have a little chat with Devin about his relationship with Molly. Surely he wouldn't continue dating her if she didn't have a strong relationship with the Lord. I knew him better than that. Right?

Opal continued working on one of the topiaries, completely silent. "Guess I never thought about it," she said finally. "I always knew Kathy went to church, but Chris did, too. So, based on external evidence, they seemed like a good fit to me."

"I think we've proven that external evidence isn't always conclusive. In order for a relationship to work, God has to be at the center of it."

She sighed. "It's been a long time since I talked to anyone about God, Annie. I'm not sure I'm ready for it yet. I still have some things to work out with Him."

"Go ahead and do that," I encouraged her. "He already knows what you're struggling with, anyway. And He wants to reason it out with you. Just know that you can't hang on to bitterness forever. If you're mad at Him. . ."

"Who said anything about being mad?" She looked at me, the lines between her eyes more pronounced.

"I'm just saying, if you're wrestling with Him over something that happened twenty or even forty years ago, then it's time to let it go. Release it. Let Him convince you that He's good and is looking out for your well-being."

"Humph." Opal rose from the table with a sigh. She took

a few steps in the direction of the refrigerator then turned back, her jaw tight. "I think it would be a good idea if we didn't talk about this anymore. It's one thing for me to drag myself out to church on a Sunday morning; another thing for you to go probing into my personal life, getting all spiritual on me."

Her words felt like a slap across the face. "I. . .I'm sorry, Opal. I'm not trying to pry. I just care about you is all. And I want you to experience a relationship that won't end badly, one you can count on. . .forever."

"Forever. Humph." As she shuffled out of the room, I heard her mutter something about her keys being lost forever and then something about how we were probably hiding her keys from her just to torment her. Go figure.

I listened as her voice faded away. One thing was sure. God had opened a door today in my relationship with Opal. For the first time, I'd captured a glimpse of what she was really dealing with. Now, if only the Lord would show me what to do with this information!

CHAPTER EIGHTEEN

BURNING EMBERS

Tuesday evening, Brandi and Scott showed up around seven to pick up Maddy. She squealed with delight when she saw them. I squealed, too. Though I loved taking care of my granddaughter, she was a handful, and I had tons of work ahead of me.

"What happened with the job?" I asked Scott.

He shrugged and then smiled. "I think the interview went well. Just pray. We'll see what God has up His sleeve."

I agreed to do just that, though I still struggled with the idea of my daughter and granddaughter moving away. What would I do without them?

I had a hard time sleeping on Tuesday night, thanks to Opal's stories about her many husbands. Though I attempted to factor this information into what had transpired at The Perfect Match, it didn't compute. Nothing she'd shared led me to believe Opal had actually played a role in burning down her own place of business. Of course, there was that one issue of the hundred and fifty thousand dollars in her savings account. She hadn't yet explained that. And what was up with that story of Max draining her dry? Didn't make sense, in light of the full bank account. Still, I couldn't find much to incriminate her beyond that. Likely O'Henry couldn't, either. I hadn't heard from him in some time.

I tossed and turned for hours, finally falling into a fitful sleep around four in the morning. Once there, I dreamed the craziest thing. In my dream, Don Quixote showed up at Louise and Nick's wedding dressed as a ring bearer. He devoured the lamb dish, right in front of the guests. A wigless Opal, dressed in an old-fashioned wedding dress, carried a packet of matches in her purse, pulling them out whenever someone drew near her. And, of all things, her ex-husband Max, the one who'd supposedly stolen money from her, turned up to claim the hundred and fifty thousand from her savings account. Teresa tagged along behind Elio Petracca, drooling like a puppy, and Chris followed behind Teresa, trying to get a great news story out of the deal.

By the time I awoke on Wednesday morning, my mind was awhirl. I had to stop thinking about this case long enough to finish up loose ends for the wedding. After all, I still had to contact the photographer, the florist, and Pastor Miller. On top of that, I had to call Janetta to check on the wedding cake and appetizers. Finally, I had to make sure Elio had a handle on the reception foods. Just thinking about the calls I needed to make exhausted me.

I took a long, hot shower, then dressed for my very busy day. By the time I got out to the kitchen, Warren had fixed me a cup of coffee and toasted a bagel, which he offered to share with me.

"You're going to need this," he said, adding a thick layer of cream cheese to the bagel.

"I am? What do you mean?"

"I mean, well. . ." He pressed the morning paper into my hand, pointing to the headline.

I zipped through the words, unable to make sense of them. " 'Another Flame Goes Out.' " I shrugged. "What is it?"

"An article about the dating service. But this one hits a little closer to home. It's about a local couple parting ways."

My blood began to boil at once. Poor Kathy! Had Chris really capitalized on his own failing marriage to get a good headline? Talk about low!

Warren pointed at the article. "I know what you're thinking, but this one isn't about Chris and Kathy. I, um, I think you'd better read it because it affects you."

Affects me?

Intrigued, I scanned the article. I could hardly believe it when I got to the line that read, *Louise McGillicuddy and Nikolas Petracca, former clients of Opal Lovelace, have decided to call it quits, just days before their wedding.*

"What?" I rose from my seat, dumbfounded. "This can't be happening. If they'd canceled the wedding, Louise would have—"

The phone rang, and I reached to pick it up, stunned when I saw the number. *Louise.* I clicked on, anxious to hear her voice. "Honey, is that you?"

I could barely make out her words through the sobbing. "It's. . .it's me, Annie. I have something to tell you."

No, I have something to tell you. Chris Brewster just flashed your heartbreak all over the morning paper. That dirty, no good, double-crossing headline monger!

"Nick and I have decided. . ." She continued on, oblivious to my thoughts. "We've decided it would be in everyone's best interest if we, well, if we called off the wedding."

I sensed her pain, of course, and my tentacles came out. I wanted to take out Elio Petracca. He was behind this; I just knew it. But why would he have gone to the paper? Was he that set on breaking my friend's heart? Making a public spectacle out of her?

"Who is *everyone*?" I asked.

She sighed. "It's not important. All that matters is. . ." She began to cry once again. "I've lost him. I've lost him, Annie. He's God's perfect man for me, and now everything is unraveling. How could this have happened? I really trusted God with this one. I felt sure I'd found Mr. Right."

I looked over at Warren, mouthing, "It's Louise." His eyes grew wide, and he took the paper in hand once again.

"I'm so humiliated," Louise said. "Everyone in town is going to have to be told. Well, everyone who's invited to the wedding, and that's pretty much the whole town. How do I go about telling our guests in such a short time?"

Um, don't worry about that. Chris Brewster has already taken care of that for you.

"I don't want to point fingers," she said, "but I have a sneaking suspicion Teresa Klein has been filling Elio's head with stories about me."

"What?" Would Teresa really do such a thing? If so, why?

"I think she's jealous that I'm happily matched and she's not found the man of her dreams."

"But what about Elio? He's interested in her, isn't he?"

"Elio's just here for six weeks, and she knows that. He's a

womanizer, no doubt about it. And likely she's already figured that out. But I really think she's turned him against me."

My mind reeled back to the can of gasoline in Teresa's car. The look on her face when I mentioned Opal's name. The trembling in her hands whenever someone talked about the fire at The Perfect Match. Had I finally found my perpetrator?

Teresa Klein. What did I know about her, really? Sure, she seemed like the quiet, sullen sort. A woman who'd never found Mr. Right. But did that make her an arsonist? Was she capable of burning Opal's place to the ground out of spite?

Only one way to know for sure. I had to find out where Teresa Klein was on the morning of the fire. . .and I needed to find out quick!

CHAPTER ⁂ NINETEEN

LIKE MOTHS TO A FLAME

By Wednesday afternoon, Opal was up to her tricks again, this time taking a walk and getting lost at the gas station on the corner of Main and Schuster. I received a call from Frank Michaels, the owner, around two in the afternoon. "Annie, you might want to come and claim Opal. She's a little turned around."

"Turned around?" The gas station was just five blocks from my house, and she'd made the trip several times before with no trouble.

"Yes, and she, well, she stole a candy bar."

"What?" Not again! Had Opal slipped over the edge? Given herself over to the dark side?

Frank laughed. "Yeah, but I let her keep it. She really seems to like Snickers bars, so I didn't make a big deal out of it. Even gave her an extra one for later."

"Gee, thanks. Feeding her habit?" I asked.

"I guess. But here's the funny part. When I confronted her about taking the candy bar, she told me she'd left a nickel on the counter. A nickel!" He laughed. "Can you beat that?"

"Hmm." No, I couldn't beat it, but I also couldn't argue with it. Snickers bars did cost a nickel at one time. The more

168 THE PERFECT MATCH

I pondered Opal's actions of late, the more I wondered if she wasn't dealing with something above and beyond what I'd initially imagined. Alzheimer's. I cringed as the word flitted through my mind.

I went and got Opal, and she waved good-bye to Frank. "He's such a nice fellow. It was pleasant to spend a few minutes talking with him. But I'm so glad you came and fetched me. Don Quixote and I must've taken a wrong turn somewhere. We got a little mixed up. Isn't that funny?"

"Happens to the best of us," I said, offering a hopeful smile.

Still, it seemed to be happening to her a lot. Especially lately. Had her crime of passion—burning down the dating service—caused her to snap? Made her a little crazy? Forgetful?

As we made the drive home, she chatted about her morning walk and all the people she'd met along the way. Nothing struck me as particularly odd until she said she'd run into Doris Schuster, our mail carrier. Doris had passed away five years ago.

Lord, what's going on here? Help me understand what's happening.

When we arrived at the house, Opal decided she needed a nap. Even Don Quixote was unusually quiet. I ushered them both off to their room, eventually peeking my head inside the door to make sure she was okay. I privately thanked the Lord that she hadn't yet heard the news about Nick and Louise. I was afraid it might drive her over the edge. Looked like she was pretty close to toppling already.

With my heart completely broken, I packed all the wedding décor into boxes then put them in the garage. My heart twisted inside as I loaded up the topiary centerpieces

I'd worked so hard on. No one would ever see them. What a waste of money and time. I spent the time praying for Louise, asking the Lord to protect her heart and give her peace. In between my prayers, however, I struggled with two things: wanting to punch Elio's lights out for ruining a perfectly good wedding, and wanting to give Chris Brewster a piece of my mind for capitalizing on it.

As I slipped the last box into the garage, I turned back with a sigh. I still couldn't believe it. The whole thing was just so sad. And so unbelievable. Just yesterday we were in full-out wedding mode. Now this. My, how quickly things could change. One minute a blazing fire. Then next, cold, dark ashes.

After returning to the living room, my thoughts shifted to the fire at Opal's place. My suspects were lining up in a tidy row. Opal stood out as the most obvious, and not just because of her odd behavior of late. The fact that she'd lied about her finances raised several red flags. Why hadn't we heard anything else from the adjuster? Or O'Henry, for that matter? Had the investigation stalled? What would it take to get it jump-started?

A couple of minutes into my ponderings, the doorbell rang. I rose from the sofa to find Sheila at the door.

"Well, hello there. Unexpected surprise."

"Hey, girl." She flashed a smile. "I thought you might want these. You left something at the church the other day. Can't believe I forgot to bring them before now."

"What?"

She held out a ring of keys, and I took them in my hand, confused.

"These aren't mine."

Sheila's brow wrinkled. "That's weird. I found them on the pew, right where you were sitting. Figured they had to be yours." She snatched them back from me then shrugged. "Oh well. I'll take them to Evelyn. Maybe she can put a notice in the bulletin next Sunday."

"Oh wait!" I smiled. "I know exactly who those belong to. They're Opal's."

"Opal's?" Sheila chuckled. "No wonder she's been walking all over town. I've had her car keys!"

"Weirder still that she took them to church at all when she didn't drive her car. There are so many things about her that leave me perplexed. You won't believe what she's done now." I filled Sheila in on Opal's antics, including the stolen Snickers bar.

"I saw her down at the bridge in the park this morning," Sheila said. "That woman really gets around. And I'll tell you what. . .seeing that cat on a leash is enough to bring a smile to any face."

I rolled Opal's keys around in my hand, an idea suddenly occurring to me. "We should use these keys to take a peek inside Opal's car."

"Where is she?" Sheila asked. "You're not worried she'll see us?"

"She's asleep. Warren's off today, but he's napping, too." I released a sigh as I mentioned my husband's name.

"Why the sigh, Annie?"

"I don't know. I'm just worried about Warren. He's been a little edgy lately, what with Opal and the animals being here. He was storming around the kitchen earlier, slamming doors and stuff. And then he did the most random thing—he suddenly decided to take the back door off and put it back on again."

"That's not as unusual as you might think. When Orin and I had a fight last spring, he painted the outside of the house."

"Oh, I thought you asked him to do that."

"Nope. I just showed up from women's group one day, and there he was, painting the house green. Wasn't my idea. But he worked out a lot of his frustrations doing something physical. Of course, I've had to live with an ugly green house ever since, but I don't complain. Have you ever heard me complain?"

About the house? No. "I guess that's what Warren's doing." I shrugged. "And who can blame him? He's put up with so much!"

"Well, you know what they say, Annie. When women are frustrated or depressed, they go shopping. When men get riled up, they invade another country. Warren's got no country to invade, so he's doing the next best thing."

"I guess." Lowering my voice, I added, "I just hope my marriage can take all of this. I love crime-solving, but I love my husband more."

"As well you should." Sheila smiled. "But I'd be willing to admit Warren's just fussing and fuming. He'll get it out of his system." She looked at the keys in my hand. "Since he and Opal are both sleeping, this looks like the perfect time for a little snooping."

"Agreed," I said. "Let's go through her car with a fine-tooth comb while she's dozing. See if we find anything suspicious."

"Ooo." Sheila clasped her hands together. "Sounds like great fun. What are we looking for?"

"Anything. Everything."

"Got it."

We tiptoed out the door and into the garage, where Opal's car had been sitting for a week and a half. As I opened the driver's side door, it let out a squeak.

"Shh!" Sheila put her finger to her lips. "We don't want to wake her up."

"I know, I know." Doing my best to be quiet, I looked around the front seat. "Nothing suspicious here."

Sheila got in on the passenger side and opened the glove box. "There's always cool stuff lurking in glove boxes. Let's see what Ms. Lovelace is up to." After pulling out the car's instruction book and a variety of receipts for tune-ups and oil changes, Sheila found something that stopped her in her tracks.

"What have we here?" She held up a tiny picture frame.

"Strange. A framed photo in the car." I reached out my hand, and she gave it to me. The smiling face in the picture looked a little like Opal, but not enough like her to think we were looking at her childhood photo or something like that. No, this young woman's picture reminded me of my own as a teen. The haircut, the way she wore her makeup. . .they were all telltale signs of the sixties.

I signaled for Sheila to exit the car. We closed the doors and locked it up, leaving the picture right where we'd found it—in the glove box. "Let me check the trunk, Sheila." I eased the trunk open, surprised to find it completely full. "Come look at this."

Sheila approached, her eyes growing wide as she saw the stash of goodies in the trunk. "What is all that stuff?"

I opened one of the boxes and unwrapped what I found inside. "Whoa. Looks like wedding china."

"My mom had china kind of like that," Sheila said. "That stuff is really old. Probably from the forties."

"Must be from her first marriage. . .when she was married to Charlie Lovelace," I observed. "Or maybe her second. But why carry it in her trunk?"

"Good question." Sheila wrinkled her nose. "Especially when the trunk smells like this. What is that?"

She fished around until she came up with a gas can from the farthest corner of the trunk on the passenger side. "Well, lookie here." Grabbing the gas can, she gave it a once-over. "I haven't seen an old gas can like this since Orin and I were first married. It's rusty. This will take you back."

It took me back, all right. Back to the morning of the fire. Back to the fact that the person who'd set the fire had used gasoline as their fuel to burn down The Perfect Match. If Opal had really raced from the burning house, as she'd told the insurance adjuster, how had she found the time to lovingly pack up her wedding china first and place it in the trunk? No, something was definitely wrong with this picture. On the other hand, if Opal had burned down her own house, would she have taken the time to save the gas can? Of course not. So much for my crazy ideas.

I closed the trunk, deep in thought.

When Sheila and I returned to the house, we found Opal awake.

"Thought maybe you'd left me," she said. "Woke up

and you were gone."

"Oh, we were just taking care of something outside." I tucked the keys in my pocket and smiled. "Everything okay in here?"

"I guess. I thought I heard doors opening and closing. Hard to sleep with people coming and going." She gave Sheila a curious look. "So, what are you doing here?"

"Well, it's nice to see you, too!" Sheila laughed. "I came by to bring you a present."

"A present?" Opal grinned. "Really? A Snickers bar?"

"No." Sheila nodded my way, and I reached into my pocket, pulling out the keys.

"Surprise!" I dangled the keys in front of her.

"I knew it!" Opal huffed. "I knew someone took my keys; just wasn't sure who to blame. It was you!" She pointed a finger at Sheila, who looked stunned.

"N—no! I found the keys on a pew at church. I brought them to Annie, thinking they were hers."

"They're mine." Opal grabbed them. "And if you don't mind, I have a few things I'd like to retrieve from my car." Clutching her kitty, she made her way out to the garage.

Sheila and I parted the miniblinds with our fingers, watching her every move.

"What do you think?" I asked Sheila. "What's she up to?"

"I think she's really not sure who to blame, but she's also mighty excited to find those keys."

A few minutes later, Opal came back in the house, holding the tiny photograph. I knew at once it held special significance, but why? Who was the girl in the picture? As Opal walked by, I took advantage of the situation to do a little fishing.

"Oh, that's a lovely frame, Opal," I started. "Would you mind if I looked at the photograph?"

She held up the black-and-white picture I'd just looked at in the car. Perhaps now she would spill her guts. . .tell me exactly what she thought I needed to hear.

Gazing at the young woman in the photograph, I decided to ask the obvious. "Who is she?"

Opal remained silent for a moment and then surprised me with her answer. "My daughter, Katy."

"Your daughter?" I could hardly contain my excitement. Opal had a daughter? Where had she been all this time? Did she even know her mother was going through the loss of her home and business? I stared at the photo once more, trying to see the resemblance between this young woman and the woman who now stood before me. Unfortunately, time had erased any one-time similarities. The woman in the picture had long hair and a smattering of freckles on her nose. "She's beautiful, Opal. I can't believe we've never talked about her."

"Well, there's a reason for that."

"Oh?" I paused, afraid to ask the obvious question. If they were estranged, it was none of my business. Only, now that Opal was living with me, maybe it was my business. Opal's voice interrupted my thoughts.

"Katy lost her battle with drugs in the sixties," she whispered.

"Oh Opal." Sheila took a seat on the sofa and gestured for Opal to join her.

I sat on the other side of Opal and looked into the innocent eyes of the young woman in the photograph. "I'm so sorry. I had no idea."

"Few people do. I was still married to Charlie—Katy's father—at the time. A lot has changed since then."

"Do you want to talk about it?"

Opal shrugged then took the frame and stared at the photo. "Do you think it's possible to miss someone more than forty years after they're gone?"

"Of course." I'd lost my grandmother when I was in college, and a knife still went through my heart every time I thought about her. I'd also lost my good friend Judy Blevins just a few years back, to cancer. It wasn't easy losing someone you loved.

"Katy was my only link to a normal life, and when she died, most of my hopes died, too."

"What do you mean. . .normal life?" I asked.

"You know, Annie. A house, a car, a family, a husband who sticks around to mow the yard and care for things. Normal. Like what you have. Like what *most* people have."

"Ah."

"No, when Katy left for the West Coast with those hippies, my version of normal left with her. And when I got the news. . ." Her voice softened and a tear rolled down her cheek. "Well, let's just say things were never the same after that." She flipped the frame over, facedown in her lap, and then shifted gears, surprising me with her words. "I'm hungry. What've you got to eat in that kitchen of yours?"

I rose from the sofa and reached over to give her a hug.

"What did you do that for?" She gave me a suspicious look.

"Because." I looked into her blue-gray eyes and smiled. "Thanks for sharing so much of your story with me. I appreciate the fact that you trust me with it."

"Mm-hmm." Not much of an answer. . .but an answer, just the same.

Suddenly I felt like cooking. "What's your favorite food, Opal?"

"My favorite?" She paused a moment then said, "Pancakes and bacon."

"This late in the afternoon?" Sheila wrinkled her nose.

Opal nodded. "Sure. I used to make 'em all the time for dinner."

"Well then, that's what we'll have," I agreed. "Come on with me to the kitchen, and I'll cook."

Sheila excused herself from our conversation and headed home. Opal shuffled along behind me as I made my way down the hall toward the kitchen.

Seconds later, Warren passed by, took one look at the relaxed expression on my face, and kissed the tip of my nose. "What are you two females up to?"

I laughed. "We're about to start cooking up a feast."

"Really?" He rubbed his stomach. "Something I might like?"

"Definitely. Comfort food," I said. "So meet us in the kitchen when the smell of what we're cooking makes you so crazy you can't stay away."

"Mmm. Now I'm curious." He gave me a wink then headed off to the office. "I'll be checking e-mails till then."

"Got it."

As we headed to the kitchen, Opal talked at length about the upcoming wedding. I didn't have the heart to tell her it had been called off. Didn't want to discourage her.

I'd no sooner pulled the eggs from the fridge than I glanced down at the table, groaning inwardly as I saw the newspaper lying there. I should've grabbed it earlier to keep the news of the wedding from Opal just a bit longer.

"Oh, the paper." She looked at me with a grin. "Let's see what big happenings are capturing the headlines today." She scanned the paper for a few moments and gasped. "Oh Annie!" With the paper still tightly clutched in her hand, she turned to me. "Is it true?"

I nodded and exhaled loudly. "It's true, Opal. I had hoped to keep it from you, actually. Meant to toss that paper in the trash where it belongs."

"Oh, I'm sick. This just breaks my heart. Those two are truly a match made in heaven. No one can deny that."

"Well, someone is trying to," I argued. "Someone pretty close to their family."

"People tearing would-be lovers apart?" Opal's expression tightened. "I know what that feels like, trust me. It doesn't feel good, let me tell you." She looked up at me. "Did Chris Brewster write this headline?"

"I guess so." With a shrug, I took the paper from her hand. "But let's don't fret about that right now, okay? What would you think about homemade blueberry syrup? I have a great recipe."

"I suppose." She read the rest of the article then stood and began to pace the room. "Oh Annie. This is awful."

"I know."

For a moment, she seemed to disappear inside herself. I watched her countenance change. . .really, truly change. It was almost as if one Opal walked out the door and another stepped in to take her place.

Doing my best to distract her, I said, "Want to come help me crack these eggs?"

"Eggs?" She looked at me with a curious expression on her face. "Why eggs?"

"Remember?" I said gently. "We're making breakfast. . . for dinner."

"Breakfast? For dinner?" She turned to me with a horrified look on her face. "Now, why in the name of all that's holy would I want to eat breakfast at dinnertime?" She walked down the hallway, muttering something about how crazy she thought I was.

Completely overwhelmed, I took the egg in my hand and gave it a harder-than-usual crack into the bowl. Watching it splat into a gushy mess felt good. Very, very good.

CHAPTER TWENTY

A MATCH MADE IN HEAVEN

On Thursday morning, I met Sheila at the gym at our usual time. I found her talking to Molly, who was using all of her youthful energy on the StairMaster. Sheila, God bless her, wasn't doing as well. She managed one step for each of Molly's two.

Though I was intrigued by whatever conversation the two of them might be having, seeing them together also put me in a bit of a jam. I'd planned to run a few things by Sheila today, including my latest suspicions about Molly. How could I do that if the two were now best friends?

I stared at my son's new love interest, picturing her actions from the security camera footage. On the morning of the fire she had gotten out of her car and. . .

"Annie! Yoo-hoo! We're over here!" Sheila waved, and I took a few steps in their direction.

"You're late, girl," she said with a grin. "But I forgive you."

Molly looked my way with a shy glance. "Good morning, Mrs. Peterson."

"Please call me Annie, Molly."

"Annie." Her cheeks flushed, and for a moment the innocent young thing reminded me of one of my own girls.

She was just a baby, and one without a family nearby. On the other hand, she was a baby who'd disguised her identity to come to a new town, and for what? To burn down a business? To steal my son?

"Devin and I went to church together last night," she said with a shy smile. "I was hoping to see you. I wanted to show you a Bible that my grandmother passed down to me. Devin said you would like that."

Oh wow. I would have liked that. Unfortunately, the migraine I'd been struggling with had prevented me from attending last night's service. And how ironic that Devin and Molly had now been to two church services together. Was the devious little vixen trying to win everyone over by coming to church? Did she think that would be enough to convince the savvy folks of Clarksborough that she wasn't an arsonist?

Slow down, Annie. Don't let these little embers turn into a forest fire. You don't know that Molly has done anything wrong. Maybe she's just an innocent girl who enjoys going to church.

"I'd love to stay and chat," I said after a moment's pondering, "but I need to run to the changing room to get into my workout clothes."

Molly glanced at the clock. "And I've got to get out of here. Work beckons." She shrugged. "I'm not complaining. I love what I do."

Yes, but what *do* you do? I wanted to ask.

I was thankful Molly left while I was changing. Sheila seemed in a sober mood by the time I stepped onto the elliptical machine.

"Packing up all the wedding stuff?" she asked. "Have they

really called it off?"

"Yes." I shook my head, thinking about poor Louise. It would be tough enough to marry someone from a completely different culture, but all the more difficult if that person's family didn't welcome you. What did Elio have against my friend, for Pete's sake? Only one way to know for sure. I would have to pay him a visit. . .and the sooner, the better.

I continued my workout, but my thoughts were elsewhere. Stopping by the restaurant on the way home from the gym made perfect sense. By the time I'd showered and dressed, I'd garnered the courage to do what had to be done. . .to say what had to be said.

I found Elio in the kitchen at Petracca's. He took one look at me and turned on his heel.

"Oh no you don't." I reached out and gently took him by the arm. "We're going to have a little chat."

"I am too busy for a chat." He grabbed a container of olive oil and a skillet. "Cooking."

"Elio." I attempted to use the kind of voice a mother would use for her son.

He sighed then set the pan down, followed by the oil. His shoulders slumped forward in defeat. "I will listen, Annie Peterson, but I must work, too." He shooed the other cook out of the kitchen then turned my way. "Say what you've come to say. Let me have it."

"I think you know why I'm here."

"Louise." His face hardened as he spoke her name.

When I nodded, he reached for an onion and a knife and began to chop. At once my eyes began stinging.

"What do you want to know?" He chopped with vigor now, and I could see the veins in his neck bulging.

"Why did you convince Nick to call off his wedding? That's all I want to know. I think Louise deserves an answer."

He continued to chop until I placed a hand on his arm. When he turned my way, I was surprised to see tears in his eyes. Were they from the pungent aroma, or had his emotions gotten the better of him?

"Annie, you don't understand. Nick is. . ."

"What?"

"He's all I have left." Elio set the knife down and leaned forward, shaking his head.

"You're right. I don't understand."

Elio paused a moment, looking down at the chopped onions. When he looked back at me, there were honest-to-goodness tears in his eyes. "You don't know our story. If you did, you would understand why Nick must come back to Athens."

"Come back to Athens? You mean he's leaving? Closing Petracca's for good?"

Elio released a sigh. "As I said, Nick is all I have left," he repeated. "My mother and father, they. . ." After a lengthy pause, he said, "They died in a car accident six years ago. And our baby brother. . ." Elio turned his back on me, and I could see his shoulders begin to heave as he wept.

"I'm sorry, Elio," I whispered. "I didn't realize you had lost your parents." A lump rose in my throat. I didn't see grown men cry very often, and this one was now weeping with full abandon.

He finally looked at me, his eyes pooling. "Joey. . .our

baby brother. . .is gone now, too."

"Oh Elio. I'm sorry."

"He was only thirty-nine. So young."

"What happened?"

Another voice rang out from behind me, startling me. "He drowned last year in a boating accident off the coast of Santorini."

I turned to face Nick, who also had tears in his eyes.

"That's why I came to America," he explained. "To get away from the ghosts of my past. But in doing so, I left behind the only family member I had left." He gestured to Elio. "I almost forgot that the love of a brother runs deeper than. . .well, than almost anything."

I paused a moment, wanting to say the right thing. While I understood their pain, at least to some extent, I couldn't see how or why this should have ended a perfectly good wedding.

"Nick, let me ask you a question." I looked him in the eye. "Do you love Louise?"

At once, he began to weep. Heavens! Two weeping men in one room. I'd never encountered such a thing, but then again, I'd rarely been in a room with two Greek men before.

"Oh Annie, you know I do!" Nick spoke through his tears. "I can't breathe without her."

"Then why. . . ?"

Elio gravitated to a nearby stool and sat, his head in his hands. "It's my doing. When I arrived, I felt sure I could convince Nick and Louise to come back to Athens with me after the wedding. It's. . .it's why I came."

"I thought you were coming to help out with the restaurant while they were on their honeymoon."

"Yes, I even arranged the honeymoon," he said with a sigh. "Don't you see? I thought if Nick took Louise to all our favorite places in Greece, she would fall in love with our homeland and want to stay. But after just a few days here, I could see her heart was here. . .in Pennsylvania. I couldn't tear her from her home. It would be wrong. But neither can I do without my brother."

"But. . ." I looked at Nick, confused. "What's wrong with the two of them staying put. . .here?"

"We have property in Athens, Annie," Nick explained. "A restaurant our father built. When I left, Joey and Elio took it on. But after Joey died. . ."

"It's just too much," Elio said. "I want to keep the memory of our father alive, but I'm just one man. I can't run the restaurant on my own." He took the dish towel and dabbed his forehead with it. "You understand?"

"Sort of. You thought Nick and Louise would come there and help you carry on what your parents started?"

He let out a lingering sigh and then nodded. "I had hoped. Our father. . .our father would have wanted his sons together. This, I know."

"But his sons can be together," I said, gesturing to the kitchen where we all stood. "And he would be thrilled that Nick has built this place and named it after him. Right?"

Elio nodded. "Well, of course. But the restaurant our father started. . ."

"Is in your hearts as much as it's in a physical place. Elio, please forgive me if I'm overstepping my bounds here, but have you prayed about this?"

"Well, I. . ."

"What if the Lord has a completely different plan in mind, one that would solve your problem, but in a different location?"

He gazed at me with a wrinkled brow.

"You cannot run the restaurant there by yourself, and Nick needs help here. This place is booming. Petracca's is full of hungry people from morning till night. Every day the line to get in the door grows longer."

"It's true," Nick said with a shrug.

"Nick's heart is here. . .with Louise and with the people of Clarksborough. And I think"—I spoke in a teasing voice—"your heart is, too."

He looked up at me with a hopeful expression in his eyes. "You think?"

"Every time I see you look at Teresa Klein, I *more* than think. I *know*." Pausing, I tried to put together my next few words. They had to be just right. "Elio, would it be such a tragedy to close down the restaurant in Athens and join your brother here?"

A look of pain came over him for a moment. Then, after a few seconds, he turned my way with a shrug. "I don't want to destroy what our father began. You see?"

"I see all too clearly. And I totally agree. But as much as your father loved that restaurant, I guarantee he loved his boys even more. And now that Joey is gone. . ." This time I got a lump in my throat. "Now that Joey is gone, you two have got to stick together. Why not do that, right here in Clarksborough? This is the perfect place for new beginnings."

Nick looked at his brother with hope in his eyes. "It would be a wonderful thing, Elio, to have you here permanently."

"I don't know. I will have to think about this." Elio rose and began to pace.

At that moment, a singsongy voice rang out. "Yoo-hoo. Anybody here?" Teresa popped her head in the kitchen door. The minute she laid eyes on Elio, her face broke into a smile. "Oh, I'm so sorry! Didn't mean to interrupt. Just thought maybe. . .well, I was hoping I could persuade you to leave the restaurant for a few minutes to take a walk through town. The lilacs are in full bloom today, and I know you told me they remind you of the ones in Athens."

If I could've burst into song at that moment, I would have. I had never witnessed such perfect timing in all my life. Teresa paused, looking at the tears in Elio's eyes, then approached him, taking his hand. "What's wrong? Have I said something to upset you? I. . .I just wanted to spend time with you while you're here." Her eyes filled with tears, too.

Good gravy. It's a cry-fest.

Elio gave her a tender look and squeezed her hand. "I will walk with you, Teresa. There are some things we must discuss."

"Oh?" She gave him a worried look, and he reached to hug her.

After a moment, Elio rose from his seat and approached me. As he drew near, he dried his eyes with his apron and leaned over to embrace me. "You are a wise woman, Annie Peterson. And perhaps we will finish this conversation when I return from my walk with this beautiful lady. In the meantime, I believe you and Nick have work to do."

"We. . .we do?" I attempted a nervous smile. "So the wedding is back on?"

"Elio. . ." Nick's expression brightened. "I wouldn't hurt you for anything in the world. You are my only brother. Are you sure. . . ?"

"I am a selfish, foolish man," Elio said. "Trying to come between a man and the woman he loves. You have my blessing, Nick. Now go and find Louise before it's too late."

"Do you mean it, Elio?" Teresa asked. "You've come around to my way of thinking after all? You're not going to try to stop Nick from marrying Louise?"

So Teresa wasn't trying to tear Louise and Nick apart, after all. Very interesting.

Elio gave her a smile then looked back and forth between Teresa and me. "You Pennsylvania women have a way of wearing a man down. That's all I have to say. Just don't tell anyone back in Greece that a woman changed my mind. They will ridicule me, to be sure!"

I'd just turned to walk out of the kitchen when something occurred to me. I turned back to look Teresa in the eye, ready to ask a question I should've just come out and asked days ago. "Teresa, on the morning of the fire. . ."

"Yes?"

"Where were you when the fire broke out?"

She shrugged. "Oh, that's easy. It was communion Sunday, my week to prepare the communion trays."

"Wait. You mean you were up at the church all morning?"

"Well, from seven forty-five on. I was with Evelyn in the kitchen. Why?"

"Oh nothing." With a wave of my hand, I turned and took a few steps toward the door. "Nothing at all."

As I left the restaurant, I felt as if I'd lost a hundred pounds.

With the Lord's help, I'd managed to convince Elio to let his brother live his own life, and I'd eliminated a suspect.

Now, off to find Louise! I had a wedding to pull off. . .in less than forty-eight hours!

CHAPTER ▌▌▌▌ TWENTY-ONE

THE HEAT IS ON

Thursday was spent in "scurry" mode. Louise and I rushed from place to place, double- and triple-checking everything. I was gone from the house for hours on end but finally returned around five thirty. From outside the front door, I could hear angry voices inside.

Hmm. It might be better if I just tiptoed away. I pressed my ear to the door, trying to decipher the noises. Warren and Opal were going at it in a major sort of way. From the sound of things, I needed to get inside, pronto.

I'd no sooner entered the house than Warren approached me with his fists clenched. I'd never seen him so worked up.

"She hit me," he said, the veins in his neck bulging as he pointed at Opal.

"I beg your pardon?"

His voice trembled as he repeated the words I'd refused to believe the first time. "Opal hit me. With her cane."

"No way. She has a cane?"

"Yes, she has a cane, and she knows how to use it. As a weapon." His hands shook, and I could read the anger in his eyes. Who could blame him? "I was coming down the hallway, and I guess I was in her way. So she took her cane and hit my legs just below the knees."

I clamped my hand over my mouth, unsure of what to say. I could hardly imagine the elderly, white-haired Opal assaulting my husband.

"Annie, I'm a patient man."

"I know you are, honey."

"Three dogs, a cat, and an elderly woman. . ." He didn't say anymore. He didn't need to.

"I'm sorry. This is all my fault. But Warren, I think this latest incident points to something bigger. I'm starting to wonder if maybe Opal. . ."

"Opal what?" An angelic voice interrupted us. "Are you wondering if I ate the last brownie?"

I turned around to face a genteel, smiling woman leaning on a beautiful hand-carved cane. "What?"

"I confess!" She giggled. "I ate the last brownie then washed out the dish and hid it in the pantry so you wouldn't notice. Is that what you two were talking about? Do I need to bake up a new batch? I love working in the kitchen, honey. I don't mind a bit." She hobbled over to the cabinet to the right of the stove and pulled out a mixing bowl. "Do we have enough eggs?"

I must admit, I toyed with the idea of cracking an egg over her head. However, in an effort to keep the peace, I reached into the fridge, handed her the eggs, and then turned to leave the room.

"You go on, honey," she crooned. "Don't worry about me. You go solve a crime or plan a wedding or whatever it is you do."

Warren muttered all the way into the next room. I could still hear him as he traipsed down the hallway toward the office. With tensions mounting, I had to wonder just how long we could go on with Opal in the house. Would he ask me to oust her. . .permanently? Or would he, perhaps, oust me?

I turned back to Opal, unsure of what to say. Half the time, she came across as nasty and rude. The other half—like now, for instance—she was practically best friend material. As she worked on the brownies, I mustered up the courage to do something I should've done ages before.

"Opal, I've got to ask this question. It's been weighing heavy on my heart for over a week now. Did you. . ." I swallowed hard then tried again. "Did you have anything to do with the fire at your building?"

Opal stopped stirring the batter and leaned forward over the bowl. I couldn't see her face from where I was standing, but the heaving shoulders let me know tears had started. Oh dear. Before long, the sobbing was gut wrenching. I'd already experienced more than my share of tears today. Now this?

I wondered if perhaps these were tears of relief at finally having been caught. She turned to face me, mascara running down her wrinkled cheeks. When she spoke, her words caught me off guard.

"Oh Annie. I'm so upset that you could think that of me!" More weeping and wailing followed. "Is that what you've been thinking this whole time. . .that I burned my own place down?"

"Well, honey, I'm sorry, but it's the case-solver in me. I can't rest till I get to the bottom of something, and I haven't been able to figure out who would do this to you, so I had to at least consider the fact that you might've done it to yourself . . .to get the insurance money."

Opal shook her head. "No, nothing could be further from the truth. And. . ." She drew in a deep breath, her gaze shifting to the floor. "I *have* money, Annie. Lots of it. I could've rebuilt that place in a heartbeat."

Okay, now we were getting somewhere.

"You have money?" I did my best to act surprised at this news.

"Yes." She nodded. "You remember telling me about the Sonniers at the church? The people you know who are related to James, my last husband?"

"Yes, of course."

"Well, I might as well up and tell you. . .the reason I went to your church last Sunday was to see if I could find them. I've avoided them for years, but I figured enough time had passed, maybe we could talk civilly. Get to the bottom of something that's been eating away at me for years."

"Opal, I'm sorry, but you've lost me completely. Could you start at the beginning and just tell me the whole story?"

After putting the filled brownie pan into the oven, she plopped into a chair and reached to scoop up Don Quixote. "I was only married to James for two and a half years before he passed. I told you that part already. And I told you that he took a lot of flack from his family for marrying me in the first place because I was divorced. What I didn't tell you was this—he left me a considerable amount of money when he died. I didn't come into the marriage with much— you'll remember I said Max pretty much took me for everything I was worth."

"Right." I paused, not sure of what to say next.

"Some people in James's family saw me as a gold digger, I guess. Thought I was marrying James for his money. But I never really cared about all that—while we were married or after I lost him."

"Why would anyone care if he left you his money anyway?" I asked. "Did he have children from a previous marriage or something?"

"No. His first wife was deceased, so that money rightfully came to me when he passed. But his siblings—there were two of them at the time—wanted it for themselves. We, um . . .well, we had a few words after James died, but the law was on my side, and they knew it."

"No doubt." My mind reeled as I thought about this. "But you won out? All of the money stayed with you?"

"Sure." She shook her head. "But here's the crazy part. And I'm sure you'll think I'm nutty for this, but other than the money I used to pay for James's funeral, I haven't spent a penny of that money in all these years."

"No way." Well, that explained the hundred and fifty thousand dollars in the bank.

"Nah." She laughed. "I check the balance every now and again to see if it's earning interest but haven't had a need for it. Till now."

"Will you use it now?" I asked. "To rebuild?"

"Well, that depends on whether or not the insurance pays." She shook her head. "And Annie, I can see how people might suspect me. I let the building fall down around me, didn't keep it up like I should have. That was more an issue of losing heart than anything financial. But I'm telling you the truth here. I had nothing to do with that building burning down. I didn't need the money then, and I don't really need it now."

Suddenly I knew in my knower that she was telling the truth. Opal hadn't set fire to her building. *Thank You, Lord. I don't have a pyromaniac living in my home!*

"I've been thinking a lot about this." She bit her lip, not saying a word for a moment. When she finally spoke, her words startled me. "Both of James's siblings have passed, but I've been thinking about giving some of that money to their kids."

"What?"

"Yes." A lone tear trickled down her cheek. "I don't have any family of my own, and I know they've got kids to support. So I'm thinking I'll keep half of it and split the other half between them."

"Opal." I didn't know what to say, other than the obvious. "You don't owe them that."

"I know." She paused, and then the tears began. "But don't you see? I'm alone. I have no one. No one. So, what's the point of having money—or things—if you have no one to share them with? It's not like I have what you and Sheila have."

"What do you mean?"

"Isn't it obvious? I guess I can say it, Annie. I'm. . .I'm jealous."

Her words sent a knife through my heart. "Jealous? Of what?"

"You. You have an amazing family. Three great kids. A

wonderful husband who loves you."

I could hardly believe her words. After a moment of reflection, I looked into her tear-filled eyes. "Can I ask you a question?"

"Well, sure."

"If you think my husband's such a peach, why did you hit him with your cane?"

"Hit him?" A dazed look came over her. "I hit him? With a cane?"

"Not ten minutes ago, according to Warren."

"How very odd. I don't recall that." She began to tremble. "Oh Annie, it's happening again."

"What?"

"I. . .I can't remember." Her gaze shifted downward. "It just keeps happening, you see. I don't know what's wrong with me lately. I'm getting so forgetful in my old age. But I didn't mean to hurt Darren."

"Warren." *She's in worse shape than I thought.*

Opal bit her lip. "I didn't mean to hurt *Warren*. He's been so kind to take me in. You all have. You're such a wonderful family." She released a sigh. "Maybe, deep down inside, I didn't want you to be happy if I couldn't be." Her eyes misted over, and within seconds mine did, too. "And as far as your children go. . .I told you about my only daughter. "

"Right."

"It just doesn't seem fair that some families are so. . .blessed and others struggle so much. I'm tired of being alone. Tired of struggling. I'm ready for someone to ease my burdens for a while."

"Oh Opal. . ." I paused a moment, finally ready to have

the heart-to-heart I'd been waiting on all this time. "Don't you see? That's that I've been trying to tell you. I only know of one person in the universe who's capable of easing burdens."

"What do you mean?"

"This is what I've been trying to tell you all along. You're in the happily-ever-after business, but there's really no happily ever after without a relationship with God."

She gave me an inquisitive look, as if she didn't quite trust my words.

"You're looking for the perfect match?" I asked her. "He's it, honey. Not a man. God. The Creator of the universe. He's the man of your dreams. He's the one who won't leave you or forsake you. And until you take His hand in yours, any other relationship will be lacking."

"Oh Annie." She shook her head. "I don't know. God and I aren't even on speaking terms, remember? How can I reconnect with someone I'm not even talking to?"

"He's been speaking to you all along, Opal," I responded. "Maybe you didn't recognize His voice, but He's been right there, whispering words of love over you."

Her eyes brimmed over once again. "Y–you think so?"

"I know so. You've shared the best kind of love possible between a husband and wife, but I promise you, there's a relationship that makes that one pale in comparison. God wants to show you just how lovable you are to Him."

"Me?" She was crying in earnest now. "Oh Annie, not me. I'm a wrinkled old woman. No one wants me. I'm just. . . like an old shoe folks have cast aside. And I'm certainly not lovable."

"Opal!" I could scarcely believe her words. "Why would you say that?"

"Think about it, Annie." She shook her head. "I wasn't acceptable to a whole church full of people when James fell in love with me. No one even tried to understand. They just heard the word *divorced* and decided to become my judge and jury instead. And I've found over the years that church folks are the worst at pointing fingers. And from what I can see, they're no more perfect than I am."

"None of us are perfect," I said. "That's why we need a Savior. But as far as people passing judgment, I can assure you, the people I know at Clarksborough Community Church are some of the most loving, accepting people I know. And Opal, many of them have been through what you have, so why would they point fingers?"

"Humph." She crossed her arms, looking as if she didn't quite believe me.

"It's true. We have people who've been wounded by divorce. People who are widowed. People who've been through rough times emotionally. People who've been taken advantage of. What you're describing is the body of Christ. Wounded. Scarred. Battered. Bruised. Neglected. Hurting. People. . .just like you and me. You've been looking for a family? Let us be that family."

She shook her head, her eyes narrowed. "I could never fit in that family, trust me."

Suddenly—in an instant—I understood Opal's behavior over the past few weeks. She'd deliberately been trying to ostracize us. To force us to reject her, so that she could prove to herself that she didn't fit in. But I would change that stinkin' thinkin' if it was the last thing I did. "Opal, I haven't talked much to you about the Bible. Maybe I should have.

But everything you're telling me reminds me of a verse I read just this morning."

She quirked a brow but didn't respond.

"The verse was First Peter, chapter one. I think it was the sixth verse. Maybe the seventh, too." I began to quote the verse I'd worked so hard to memorize: " 'In this you greatly rejoice, though now for a little while you may have had to suffer grief in all kinds of trials. These have come so that your faith—of greater worth than gold, which perishes even though refined by fire—may be proved genuine and may result in praise, glory and honor when Jesus Christ is revealed.'

"We have to go through the fire in order to be refined," I explained. "To be pure gold. Sure, it's not fun going through trials or grief. But we're strengthened when we've been through the fire." *Lord, I get it now. You've been refining me so I'd know what to say to Opal when the time came. Thank You for that.*

"Well, I've been through it all right." Opal slumped down in her chair. "And I've had my share of grief and trials. Maybe that's why I've worked double time to match folks up," she said with a sigh. "To prove I'm good at something. But it looks like I'm a failure at that, too."

"Oh, I don't think so. You got it right with Louise and Nick. And you pegged Devin and Molly."

I'd no sooner spoken Molly's name than a shiver ran down my spine. If both Teresa and Opal had been eliminated as suspects, that meant I was down to two: Molly and Chris. If I could just get through this wedding, I would definitely have to pinpoint one. . .or the other.

CHAPTER ▮▮▮ TWENTY-TWO

LITTLE DROP OF WATER

Thursday evening, after a whirlwind of a day, Warren, Opal, and I settled down at the kitchen table for our evening meal. I'd finally managed to share Opal's story with Warren, and the two of them seemed to be getting along. For now. For that matter, even the animals seemed to have declared a truce. Of course, there was that one little incident with the neighbor, who claimed Opal had stolen her mother's cane, but we'd ironed that out with little difficulty.

In fact, I had the strangest feeling the Lord had swept in and taken charge of pretty much everything.

We were in the middle of dinner when Opal started giggling.

I looked up from the plate of meat loaf she had cooked, curious. "What is it, honey?"

"Oh, I just thought of something. Now that the wedding's back on, I can give Louise her gift."

"You bought her a gift?"

Opal shook her head. "No, I didn't buy it. It's something I've had for sixty years."

"Sixty years?" Warren looked at her, stunned. "What is it?"

"My wedding china set."

Immediately, relief washed over me like an ocean wave. The china! That explained it!

"I wrapped it up weeks ago and put it in my trunk," she explained. "I've had every intention of finding the perfect box to put it in, but never found the time. . .what with the house burning down and all." She looked at me with a woeful expression. "Will you help me find a box after we're done eating, Annie?"

"I'd be honored."

She began to share all the details of the china, mesmerizing us with her story. Turns out the pattern dated back to the late 1800s and had Greek roots. Would Louise ever get a kick out of this gift!

I had just started to clear the table when the phone rang. I answered and heard my son-in-law's breathless voice.

"Mom?"

I could tell something was wrong. "What happened, Garrett?"

"I'm at the hospital with Candy."

"What?" A thousand questions ran through my mind. "What happened to her? Was she in an accident?"

"No, nothing like that. She's fine. We were at Petracca's and she fainted. It's the second time in a week."

"Second time?" How come I hadn't heard about the first time?

"She didn't want to worry you," Garrett said, as if reading my thoughts. "But she's okay. The ambulance brought her up to the emergency room to be checked out. Can you meet us here?"

"Are they keeping her?"

"They're just observing her for a couple hours, but I think she'd feel better if her mom came."

"I'm on my way."

Warren and I jumped into the car and raced toward the medical center. More questions ran through my mind. "If she's been struggling with fainting spells, why wouldn't she tell us?" Suddenly I remembered that she'd given me clues all along. That day at the salon, she'd complained of feeling weak, hadn't she? And a couple of other times, she'd been off her game. But to faint and not tell her mama? What was wrong with that girl?

I went through a verbal litany of illnesses that could've caused two fainting spells in a week's time, low blood sugar topping the list. I turned to Warren, who gripped the steering wheel for dear life.

"She's not eating right. I've tried to tell her. And she's on her feet all day. We talked about this when she was doing my hair."

"She's probably just overworked," Warren said, obviously trying to keep his voice steady. "Let's wait to hear what the doctor has to say, Annie. And we'll pray."

He began to usher up a passionate prayer, right there in the car. By the time he finished, I felt much better.

We arrived at the hospital, and I rushed to see my girl. I found her sitting up in bed eating a small container of ice cream. She glanced my way with an I'm-sorry-I-bothered-you smile.

"They're letting you eat?" I sat on the edge of the bed. That was a good sign, for sure.

"Yes, the doctor said I needed to eat something. I haven't been keeping much down over the past week or so."

"Well, I wish you'd told me. You've probably got that bug that's going around. Either that, or it's your blood sugar. Sometimes people faint or get nauseated when their blood sugar drops. I've told you that you need to take better care of yourself. Eat better. Stay off your feet."

"Mom, slow down." Candy grinned. "My blood sugar is perfect. Other than being a little anemic, I'm in tip-top shape."

"Anemic?" *Hmm.* Well, I could see how that might cause fainting. Maybe.

Candy looked at Garrett and grinned. "You want to tell them, or should I?"

At once, my fears lifted. *Oh, you little stinker! You're. . .*

"Pregnant!" She laughed until she almost cried. "We're pregnant. Five weeks. I just had my first ultrasound."

Warren let out a whoop and reached to slap Garrett on the back. I did what any good mother would do—erupted in tears.

"You didn't know?" I asked.

"Nope. I've been so irregular for the past several months, I never thought about it. And it's not like we were trying. We weren't. I guess this little one is a surprise package."

"Oh honey, I'm so happy. So very, very happy." Candy was going to be a mama. Candy, the one who didn't know how to bathe, change, or feed a child. *Hmm.* Looked like we had a lot of work to do.

Just then a knock at the door interrupted us. I glanced up, stunned to see Devin and Molly. The minute I laid eyes on her, my heart started racing. *Be still, Annie. Don't let her see that you're anxious.*

"Uncle Devin!" Candy squealed.

"What?" He looked at her, clearly stunned. "I come in here thinking you're dying, and it's 'Uncle Devin'?"

Candy nodded then grinned. "That's the verdict. Unless you want me to ask for a second opinion or something."

"Oh, I think it's wonderful," Molly said, her eyes now twinkling. "You're going to be a great mom, Candy. And if the baby looks anything like the two of you, he or she is going to be gorgeous."

Man, can this girl schmooze. She's pouring it on really thick. What is she really getting at?

"Aw, thanks." Candy blushed. "You're so sweet." She patted the edge of her bed, encouraging Molly to come and sit with her. When she did, Candy took her by the hand. "I don't know why, but I feel like I've known you forever, like you've always been a part of our family. I know we don't really know each other, but I hope that will change. You seem like our kind of people."

Hmm. I wasn't so sure about that, though I did have to agree that we didn't know Molly very well.

Suddenly an idea came to me, one that would give me a chance to see if Molly really was who she said she was.

I turned to Candy with the most casual look on my face I could muster. "So, what baby names are you thinking of?"

"Wow, I don't know." Candy looked at Garrett. "This is all so new. I never even thought about the fact that everyone needs a name."

"Well, of course they do. Everyone needs a name." I

turned to Molly and gave her a pointed look. "Your name is your signature. It's who you are." Shifting gears, I said, "And this baby will be your first, so you need to think of something really special."

"I heard about a woman named Ima Hogg," Garrett suggested. "We could go that route. Give him—or her—a name that matches our last name of Caine."

"Well, I've already got the best one," Candy said with a grin. "I'm Candy Caine, after all. So what should our little Caine be?"

We went back and forth, offering suggestions. Finally I turned the tables, ready to stir up a little fire under Molly. "Forget about trying to match up the first name with the last. If it's a girl, why don't you name her something lyrical, something like. . .Brenna."

As I spoke the word, Molly slowly turned her head, our eyes locking. For a second, I thought she might crack, but she managed to wipe the "I've just been caught" look from her face and return to the conversation as if nothing out of the ordinary had happened.

"I've always loved that name," Molly said with a grin. "It means 'little drop of water' in Gaelic."

Every eye in the room turned to her.

"How did you know that?" Candy asked.

"Oh, that's easy. Brenna is my middle name." Molly beamed with joy.

My heart immediately plummeted to my toes. *She really is Brenna?* Maybe the Ratcliff part was right, too. But how? And why?

Candy's face lit up with this revelation. "Oh wow, I just

love learning the meaning behind names."

I gazed at Molly's innocent face again. "So your middle name means 'little drop of water'?"

When she nodded, my mind reeled back to the picture I'd seen of Molly getting out of her car next to Opal's building.

I just had to wonder if that "little drop of water" was going to be enough to put out a great big fire.

CHAPTER ‖ ‖‖‖ TWENTY-THREE

A MATCHED SET

The Friday morning headline took us all by surprise. When I read the words ARSON INVESTIGATORS CLOSING IN ON SUSPECT IN LOCAL FIRE, my heart gravitated to my throat. No way! Someone else had figured out who set the fire? The investigators had beaten me to the punch? While I was thrilled to think there might be an end in sight for Opal, it did disappoint me a little that I'd fallen down on the job.

I sat down at the kitchen table to read the article, expecting it to pinpoint Molly. Instead, I gasped as I read Chris Brewster's inflammatory piece slam-dunking Opal! "Heavens to Betsy!" I looked at Warren as he came in the room. "Honey, I think you'd better read this. According to the paper, we've got a criminal living in our home."

"A criminal?" Opal's voice rang out as she entered the kitchen behind Warren. "What does that paper say, Annie? Are they blaming. . .me?"

Before I could respond, she snatched the paper from my hand and read the story. When she finished, her eyes were filled with tears. "Who does he think he is, saying all that about me? No one has proven anything, and yet Chris

Brewster has pointed his ugly finger my way. Everyone in town is going to suspect me now." She paced the room, carrying on at lightning speed. Not that I blamed her. Chris's words angered me, too.

Warren took the paper and read the story. As he did, Opal and I talked about our options. "Why don't we do this, honey?" I said. "I've been working for nearly two weeks to figure this out. I know you didn't do this. And I'd be willing to bet O'Henry knows it, too. Why don't you work with me to figure out who really did it?"

"Ooo!" Opal's eyes lit up. "You mean, I can be a super sleuth, too?"

"Sure. Why not? We'll crack this case wide open and prove to everyone in Clarksborough that you didn't set that fire. And we'll find the one who did, too!" As I spoke the words, I immediately thought of Molly. "And I know just where we'll start. Do you feel up to going to town?"

"Well, sure. Just let me put on my support hose and a decent dress." She winked. "Can't wait to see what you've got up your sleeve!"

Twenty minutes later, I pulled the car out of the driveway. Opal sat next to me in the passenger seat, going on and on about Chris. "I can't believe I actually helped that man find a wife. Poor Kathy. I paired her up with. . .well, with a monster!"

"I don't know if he's a monster or not, but he certainly likes to sell those papers, doesn't he?" I sighed as I thought about how he'd taken advantage of so many people over the past couple of weeks.

As I pulled into the parking lot at the cell phone store,

I turned to Opal. "Before we go inside, would you mind walking me around your property and telling me every detail of how the building was laid out? And maybe we could go over what happened the morning of the fire one more time."

"Sure."

We got out of the car and crossed the side street. As we did, my mind reeled back again to the footage I'd watched of Molly pulling her car up to this very street on the morning of the fire. A shiver wriggled its way up my spine as I thought about poor Devin. Had he locked lips—and hearts—with a criminal? If so, how would he take the news that his girlfriend was capable of arson?

For the next ten minutes, Opal and I walked the perimeter of her property, talking through every detail of the morning of the fire. I took notes, hoping something she might say would trigger something.

"I was standing here. . ." She gestured to where the kitchen window used to be. "Looking outside. Something caught my eye."

"What was it?"

"A car," she said. "It stopped on the side street. I thought maybe I had visitors." She shrugged. "But no one ever comes to see me on Sunday mornings."

"Can you tell me more about the car? Make, model?"

She giggled. "Annie, with so many newfangled cars out on the road today, you expect me to know all that?"

Gotcha. "Well, let me ask you another question, then. Did anyone knock at the door?"

"Nope." She shook her head. "I went back to feeding Don Q and never thought another thing about it. A couple minutes later I looked out the window again, and the car was gone."

"But you're sure you didn't hear anything at the back of the house?"

She shook her head. Then, a moment later, her eyes widened. "Well, come to think of it, after the car left, I heard something."

"What was it?"

She giggled. "You're going to think I'm being silly, but it was Don Q. He started acting so strangely."

"Strangely, how?"

"Well, he was sniffing at the back door. I thought he wanted to go outside, so I opened the door. When I did, I thought I saw a shadow of some sort."

"Did you tell the police?" I asked.

Opal shook her head. "No." Then, as tears rose to cover her lashes, she said, "Annie, I guess there's something you need to know about me. I mentioned it once before, but didn't really elaborate."

"What's that?"

"Well, sometimes. . ." A tear trickled down her cheek. "Sometimes I forget things."

Like where you put the creamer or your keys.

"It's been going on a few months," she said, dabbing at her eyes. "I've been so scared to tell anyone, but I'm afraid maybe I'm getting. . .senile."

"Oh honey." I wrapped her in my arms. "We all have forgetful spells. But I understand your concerns. Maybe we can check into that, to ease your mind." After a pause, I added, "But you're pretty sure you saw something outside your back door?"

"I. . .I think so." She shook her head. "Oh, I wish I could remember. It's all so fuzzy now."

"I understand, honey." I turned to face the cell phone store. "Why don't we go on into the store to visit with Adam?"

"I just love that young man," she said with a hint of a girlish giggle. "I used to take him cookies when I lived here."

"So he told me!"

We crossed the street together and entered the store to find Adam waiting on us.

"Thanks for seeing me again," I said with a nod. "Hope you don't mind that I called so early."

"Nope. I was glad to hear from you. Has something changed since we looked before?"

"No, not really," I said. "I'm just trying to piece some things together in my mind."

"Well, let's go back to my office."

As we walked through the store, Opal caught sight of a new cell phone advertisement. "Ooo, great phone. I might have to buy that one."

"You've already got the latest technology in the phone I sold you last month, Mrs. Lovelace," Adam said with a chuckle. "Why get another?"

"Well, that one didn't make it out of the fire. Besides, I just like to keep a good phone handy." Her eyes clouded over, and I looked at her closely.

"Opal, what's wrong?"

She stopped in her tracks and began to cry once more. "Annie, you never know when bad news is coming. I found out about Katy over the phone. And when Max took off with my money, I got a call from the bank saying he'd emptied my account. Seems like so much of the bad news I get is by phone."

"So. . ." I spoke gently. "You're afraid to go without a phone, for fear you'll miss a call?"

"M—maybe." She sighed. "I don't know. Is that silly? I'm always waiting on more bad news."

"Well, honey, you've had your fair share. But let's make a deal, okay? From now on, let's assume all the news will be good. Let's imagine that God's going to send you great news, in fact. Not bad."

Her face lit up with excitement. "Well, there's a new perspective! Good news is on its way!"

"And it's going to start as soon as we figure out who did this dastardly deed," I said with a grin. "So, let's get to it, Watson."

"You've got it, Sherlock!" She gave me a warm hug, and we continued our trek into Adam's office.

He was there waiting for us with the machine cued. I gestured for Opal to sit, which she did.

"Here we go again," Adam said, pushing the PLAY button.

Opal and I watched the footage from start to finish. When she saw the car approach, she pointed at the screen. "Yes! That's the car I was telling you about. But I never saw who was inside."

As we watched Molly exit the car, Opal's mouth flew open. "Oh dear! Isn't that the new deputy?"

"Yes," I said.

"Oh my goodness." Opal continued to watch as Molly walked to the back of Opal's house. "I wonder if that was the shadow I saw."

"Could be," I said. "But she doesn't stay back there very long, does she? Didn't you say Don Q wanted to go out *after* the car left?"

"Oh, that's right." She bit her lip. "At least, I think that's right. I'm not completely sure, Annie."

"It's okay, Opal. We'll get this figured out."

We watched as Molly's car pulled away from the curb. Then Adam turned to me and said, "Well, what do you think? Any red flags?"

"Actually, yes." Something had raised a couple of red flags, but not what I was expecting. Not at all. "Would you mind playing that again? And could you slow it down this time?" As the machine ran in slo-mo, I watched what was happening in the distance. Yes, right there. I'd noticed it before but hadn't thought much about it. The green car that slowly passed Molly on the street—who did it belong to? Probably just someone driving by, completely unaware. Still, it might not hurt to check.

"Would you pause the tape, please?"

As he did, I took note of the car: a green Avalon, license plates a little blurry. I made out a few of the letters and numbers, but not all. I'd have to check with O'Henry to see if he could help me track down the owner. Or, in a small town like this, just keep an eye out for it.

I thanked Adam for his help and headed out with Opal at my side. She chattered all the way. "What are you thinking, Annie? Do you think it was Molly? She looks like such a sweet thing. She. . ."

Opal stopped cold as we stepped outside the cell phone store. There, in the street next to us, Molly passed by—not in a patrol car, but in her own vehicle.

Opal grabbed my arm and pulled me behind a concrete pole. "What do you think, Annie? Is she our man?"

"I don't know." I peeked out from behind the pole to see what Molly was up to. She'd pulled her car to the side of the road. I watched as she got out and stood at the edge of Opal's property with a camera in hand. "Why are we taking pictures, Miss Molly?" I whispered. "What's your secret?"

"Let's go get her!" Opal took a step in Molly's direction, but I stopped her.

"Rule one of sleuthing is not to get caught," I told her in a hoarse whisper. "Let's just watch and see what she does."

"Humph."

Seconds later, Molly got into her car and left. Opal and I stepped out from behind the pole.

"Whew, that was close!" Opal's eyes were wide with excitement. "And so thrilling! I don't know when I've had this much fun, Annie!"

I had to laugh at that one. "Well, from now on, you're my right-hand man. And I have a feeling we're going to be quite a team, Opal Lovelace. . .er, *Watson*."

"If we solve this case, we can open our own investigative firm," she said with a twinkle in her eye. "What do you think of that, Annie?"

I think my husband would kill me.

"Let's just see if we can get this one solved first," I said finally. "But I think we're well on our way."

CHAPTER ⛩ TWENTY-FOUR

ALL-CONSUMING FIRE

I spent the rest of the afternoon making calls to O'Henry and finalizing plans for the wedding rehearsal, which was scheduled to take place at six o'clock. I gave O'Henry the information about the green Avalon, and he promised to try to track down the owner. He also promised to keep an eye on Molly.

"We investigated her thoroughly before hiring her, Annie," he insisted. "Didn't really find anything suspicious, to be honest. But I understand your concerns, and we're on the job, I promise."

"I know you think you know her," I insisted. "But who is this Brenna Ratcliff that she's pretending to be? And why has Molly been using a pseudonym at all?"

"You're basing all of this on a photograph from the Web," he reminded me. "Just keep in mind that anyone could have uploaded her photo to that site. People who join dating services often post bogus photographs because they don't want people to see what they really look like."

A wave of relief swept over me. I'd never considered that possibility. Maybe someone was just using Molly's photo without her knowledge.

At four forty-five, Opal took Don Q for a walk. I headed to my bedroom to get dressed for the rehearsal. I touched up my makeup and fiddled with my hair, growing anxious about a great many things—my suspicions about Molly, the headline about Opal, and a host of details related to tomorrow's wedding ceremony. How in the world could I possibly juggle so many things at once? I'd taken on too much!

As I looked over my to-do list one final time, my cell phone rang. Sheila's opening words made me smile.

"You're a miracle worker, Annie Peterson."

"Oh? I am?"

"Yes. I'm still reeling over the fact that you got Nick and Louise back together."

"No, hon. God did that. I just had a little chat with Elio."

"Well, I don't know what you said, but from what Evelyn tells me, Louise is like a different person. She's acting like a giddy schoolgirl."

"Well, of course she is." I grinned as I thought about the conversation I'd had with Louise yesterday afternoon. "She has a lot to be happy about. It's one thing to think people don't like you; another to find out the situation really didn't have anything to do with you at all. This was an issue between two brothers."

"Kind of like Jacob and Esau?"

"Hmm. Never thought about it, but I guess there are some similarities."

"Well, families are complicated things, aren't they? Folks don't always see how they fit—in their own families or the body of Christ, for that matter."

"Well, since you said that, I might as well tell you about Opal."

"Opal?" Sheila laughed. "Are you thinking of adopting her?"

"Maybe." I smiled, thinking of what Warren would say if I dared suggest such a thing. "But I was really thinking about what you said about the body of Christ, about people feeling like they don't fit. That's what reminded me of Opal."

I told Sheila every detail of my most recent conversation with Opal. By the end of it, I could hear the catch in her throat. "Oh Annie, I feel terrible. I'm one of those people who hasn't made her feel particularly welcome. I'm an awful person."

"No, you're just a person—like me—who's focused on her own family, her own stuff. I guess God is trying to teach us to look outside our own little circles to the people we might be missing."

"It's that good Samaritan story all over again," Sheila said.

"Yes. I have to wonder how many people I've overlooked over the years," I said with a sigh. "I've been so busy raising kids and working that I usually don't even pay much attention to what's going on in the lives of people around me. But that's going to change. If God's taught me anything in the past couple of weeks, it's that He wants me to expand my borders."

I glanced at the clock on the wall. "Speaking of expanding borders, I have to run. I told Louise I'd be at the church by five thirty. We have the rehearsal tonight, you know.

"Oh, that's right. Well, Orin and I will see you tomorrow evening at the wedding."

"Can't wait!" I flew into action, kissing my husband on the cheek as he entered the door from work and then quickly zipping out the door. I arrived at the church just in time to meet Louise in the parking lot before entering the building.

"Oh Annie! I'm a bundle of nerves!"

"It's to be expected." I did my best to calm her down as we entered the building. We chatted all the way to the fellowship hall. I looked around in shock, surprised to see youth group paraphernalia everywhere. "Wow." I did my best to divert Louise's attention, ushering her to the sanctuary, where Pastor Miller and Nick were waiting for her. Her cheeks flushed pink the minute she laid eyes on Nick. Oh, what fun this was turning out to be!

The three of them settled in to chat about the ceremony, and I found myself distracted, thinking about the condition of the fellowship hall. I'd better look around to see if I could find Evelyn. She'd know what to do.

Reentering the fellowship hall, I ran headlong into Kathy Brewster. "Hey, girl," I said, taking a few steps in her direction. "I'm happy to see you here tonight."

"Evelyn asked for my help." She gestured around the room. "As you can see, the place is still in a shambles after the youth function on Wednesday night, so I thought I'd help pull it into shape before tomorrow. And besides. . ." She sighed. "I need something to do to keep my mind off things."

"Are you still staying at your mom's place in Quakertown?" I asked.

"Yes, but I've been in Clarksborough most of the afternoon. I went by the house around four, but Chris wasn't there. I'm sure he's at the paper." She paused then shook her head. "Annie, I read this morning's headline. I feel so bad for Opal. Poor thing. She's been through so much already."

"I know. And I know for a fact that arson investigators aren't pinpointing her. I talked to O'Henry today, and he confirmed that."

"Sometimes I think Chris is desperate for a story." Her eyes brimmed with tears. "I'm sorry," she apologized with the brush of a hand. "That man is always making me cry."

"No, I'm the one who's sorry. For you."

"I feel like I've been crying ever since the morning of the fire at Opal's place."

That certainly got my attention. I glanced at my watch, wondering if I had time to hear the rest of the story. Five forty. Plenty of time.

"Chris and I had a little tiff right before church that morning," Kathy said with a sigh. "He left without me. I, um. . .well, I walked to church."

"What? He left without you?" My insides started seething at the very idea.

"Yes." She shook her head. "I didn't want anyone to know because I knew how it would make him look. But now, frankly. . ." She sighed again. "Anyway, that morning he was ready to leave a lot earlier than usual. We always stop off at Donut King to pick up donuts for the Prime Timer's class, you know."

"Oh, that's right. Orin thinks it's wonderful that Chris does that for them. Such a blessing."

"Yes." Kathy smiled. "For all his faults, Chris is really generous with the older people at the church." She wrinkled her nose then added, "But I guess it's fair to admit he's also a schmoozer. Sometimes I think he buys those donuts to get the older folks to warm up to him. They spill the beans and give him some juicy tidbits in exchange for sugar."

I laughed. "That might be a temptation for me, too. Will talk for donuts."

We had a good laugh at that one. Still, I wanted to get to the bottom of this. It felt important to know what had happened that particular morning.

Kathy grew more serious. "Anyway, on that Sunday I guess I wasn't ready in time. So he stormed around the house, saying he had to get the donuts early for some reason. Something about a special order because they were having extra people in class."

"So, when you weren't ready he just left?"

"Well, it wasn't really like that. He was supposed to come back and get me in fifteen minutes, but. . ."

"You ended up walking?"

"Yes. I waited twenty minutes, convinced he'd come back, but he never showed. I even tried him on his cell phone. No answer."

"Strange. You think he just got caught up in what he was doing and forgot?"

"Well, that's what I asked him when I finally got to church. But the service was already starting, so we couldn't really get into it till afterwards. That's when I gave him a piece of my mind." A look of remorse let me know how she felt about that now. "I know a lot of people saw us arguing, and I ended up apologizing to him because I put him on the spot. I always hate it when these private issues seep out in public like that."

"Well, we all argue, honey." I thought of Warren at once. He wasn't the type to openly argue, but we'd had our moments.

"I don't want people to think badly of Chris, that's all. He's a great guy. He really cares about those Prime Timers."

"Oh, I'm sure."

Still. . .something Kathy had said left me feeling sick inside. Her husband had been so concerned about buying donuts that he'd made her walk to church? What kind of man would do something like that to his wife? I knew Chris was mean-spirited, but why go so far to prove a point?

Her story left me feeling uneasy all the way around. Several things about it just didn't make sense. Maybe if I could get this wedding behind me, I'd be able to think more clearly about what had happened that morning. For now, I'd better shift into wedding coordinator gear. Louise needed me!

CHAPTER **⌗⌗⌗⌗⌗** TWENTY-FIVE

YOU'VE MET YOUR MATCH

On Saturday afternoon, I arrived at the church two hours before the wedding ceremony was set to begin. First order of business. . .check the sanctuary. The candelabras needed to be set in place, and I'd noticed last night the unity candle was a little off-kilter, too. After straightening that out, I turned my attention to putting bows on the pews where the family members would be seated. Then I headed off to the bride's room to make sure Louise would have a full-length mirror to dress in front of.

That done, I scurried off to the fellowship hall, hoping it had been cleared of all youth group debris and that the tables had been set up. I smiled when I saw the rows of tables adorned with beautiful white tablecloths. *Thank you, Evelyn and Kathy. I owe you.* I put the centerpieces in place, checked on the buffet table, then turned my attention to the head table, where the bride and groom would sit. This was always my favorite part—adding flowers and ribbon to the head table. Making it special for the happy couple.

Warren and Pastor Miller joined me a few minutes later with chafing dishes in hand. I directed them to the buffet table, though I had to wonder why I hadn't seen or heard from Janetta yet about the cake and the food. Usually she showed up earlier than this. At six o'clock, with only an hour to spare before the big event, I still hadn't seen Louise, either. Pulling off a wedding without a caterer was one thing, but I'd never managed a wedding without a bride before.

We traded a couple of text messages, and I breathed a sigh of relief when I got the news that Louise was on her way. At five minutes after six I stepped outside in the courtyard to have a look around.

I noticed her car pulling in at that very moment. I waved and smiled.

Seconds later, Louise approached with a broad smile on her face, her wedding dress in hand. "Annie, I'm so excited! I can't believe this is finally happening!"

Teresa stood at her side, beaming. "Did you hear our news? Elio is staying. . .for good. And we're dating."

Louise took Teresa's hand and squeezed it. "I hope you don't mind a little impromptu change to the ceremony, Annie, but I've asked Teresa to stand up with me." She gave Teresa a wink. "Maybe someday soon I can do the same for her."

"Mm-hmm." I gave her a grin, but just as quickly, my smile faded. In the far corner of the parking lot I noticed a green car pulling in. Squinting, I tried to make out the make and model. My heart quickened as I realized what I was seeing. A green Avalon. *Suddenly I was a jumble of nerves. Not today! Not here! Not now!*

"We'll be inside," Louise said, reaching to give me a hug. "Can you meet us in the bride's room in a few minutes,

Annie? I have something I want to give you."

"Of course. I can't wait, honey!"

As the ladies made their way inside, I watched the green car. Trying to act casual, I stepped to the side of the building then reached in my purse for my cell phone. I punched in O'Henry's number, giving him a frantic 911 version of the events unfolding before me. He promised to come ASAP.

As I rounded the side of the building once more, I ran headlong into Chris Brewster. "Oh Chris." I put my hand on my chest in an attempt to slow my now-rapid heart rate. "You scared me to death!"

"Me?" He grinned. "How come? What did I do?"

"Oh, I was just. . ." I stopped cold as I realized what had happened. The green Avalon. It was Chris Brewster's car. I'd never paid attention to it before, but. . .it had to be.

Just then, Warren stuck his head out the fellowship hall door. "Annie, want to come in here and check these tables?"

"Um, sure." *Right after I figure out how to keep Chris here till O'Henry comes.*

"We could use some help inside," I said, turning back to Chris. "Would you mind?"

He shrugged. "Why not?"

Chris traipsed along on my heels as we entered the fellowship hall. I tried to mouth, "Oh, help!" to Warren, but I could tell from the expression on his face he couldn't read my lips. I forced a smile and prayed for the Lord's guidance and protection.

Just then Louise stuck her head out of the bride's room. "Do you have a minute, Annie?"

"Oh, I. . ." Man! My attentions were torn, but this day was

all about the bride, not about catching would-be criminals. Besides, I didn't have any proof Chris had done anything wrong. I smiled at Louise and said, "Let me check the tables for Warren, and I'll be right back."

When I turned around from speaking to Louise, I was surprised to find Devin and Molly standing there talking to Chris.

"Hey, you two are early." I looked at Molly in her beautiful green dress and ivory blazer. That innocent face. Those darling freckles. Then I looked at Chris with his narrowed eyes. His deceptive smile. *Heavens to Betsy! I'm standing in the presence of an arsonist, but I don't know which one to choose. . . Molly or Chris!*

"Can I help, Annie?" Molly asked, her eyes sparkling with excitement.

"Sure. Could you and Devin find the chair covers? Maybe you two and Chris could take care of those before the guests arrive."

"Chair covers?" Chris looked doubtful. "I'll just take notes."

"For your next article?" I quipped.

Warren gave me a warning look, and I turned on my heel. Better get back to Louise's room before I did something to blow this case wide open. . .right here in the fellowship hall.

On the way down the hall, I passed Roger Kratz, one of my favorite senior citizens. He paused to shake my hand. "How are things going at your place, Annie?" he asked. "Is, um. . .well, is Opal still staying with you?"

"She is." I nodded, curious.

"Oh, well that's nice. That's nice." He continued on his

way down the hall.

Lord, are You doing a little matchmaking of Your own? The very idea made me want to laugh.

When I got to Louise's room, Teresa had already started helping her into the beautiful dress. Though my hands trembled uncontrollably, I did my best to offer assistance.

"You okay, Annie?" Louise looked my way with a smile. "I think you're more nervous than I am."

"Oh, I'm fine." I gave her hand a gentle squeeze. "Just fine." After we helped her button the beautiful ivory gown, I let out a whistle. "Louise McGillicuddy, I daresay you're about the prettiest thing I've ever seen."

"Oh Annie. . .stop." Her cheeks flushed pink.

"No, I mean it. You're a beautiful bride. And I can't wait for Nick to see you. He's going to flip."

"You think?" she asked.

"I know."

Teresa busied herself fixing Louise's hair into an upswept "do." "I'm sure it's not as lovely as it would have been if Candy could have done it," she said, "but I used to be pretty good at fixing hair, back in my day."

"I think it looks perfect." Louise gave Teresa's hand a squeeze. "It's just the way I pictured it."

I gave Teresa a wink. "Maybe Candy will give you a job at the salon. You never know."

"Really?" Teresa's eyes lit up. "Wouldn't that be something?"

Louise looked my way and giggled. "Almost ready now. Just one more thing to take care of." She pointed to her purse. "Annie, would you get my bag? I have something for you."

I reached for the purse and handed it to her. She opened

it and lifted out a tiny gift box, which she pressed into my hand.

"Go on. Open it."

With my hands still vibrating, I opened the box. I smiled when I saw the necklace inside.

"It's the Greek letter *A*," she explained. "*A* for Annie and *A* for new beginnings. Alpha. Get it?"

"Yes!" *The Alpha and the Omega, the Beginning and the End.* "I remember. And. . .and I love it." Pulling the delicate gold chain from the box, I slipped it on and fastened the clasp. I fingered the beautiful gold charm and smiled. "I've never had anything like it, Louise. It's amazing."

"I'm glad you like it."

Teresa looked at me with a worried expression on her face. "Oh dear. I forgot the hair spray."

"Oh, no worries. I have some in my car."

Perfect time to escape to the parking lot to see if O'Henry had arrived. I slipped past the others in the fellowship hall and made my way to my car. No sooner had I reached for the hair spray than I heard a car pull in next to me. O'Henry stepped out, nodding. "Annie."

"Glad you're here. I'm a nervous wreck." I filled him in on Chris's whereabouts then followed on his heels as he entered the church.

We found the others hard at work. Well, all but Chris, who stood off to the side, talking on his cell phone. Wait. Was he talking to someone or about someone? Sounded more like he was taking notes, recording the goings-on in the room. But why? Surely he wouldn't write about the wedding. It wasn't headline material, right?

O'Henry nodded in Molly's direction, and she approached with a whisper. "Ready to roll?"

"Huh?" What were these two up to?

"We've been watching Chris for days, Annie," Molly explained. "But that footage was just what we needed to place him at the scene of the crime. Up till then, we just had some suspicions based on his headlines and a few things he's said to others. No physical evidence."

"Are you saying he. . .are you really. . .do you mean. . . ?"

Molly nodded, and O'Henry confirmed with a brusque, "Yup. Now we've got some work to do. We've got to get him away from the others. Can one of you ladies corral him in the kitchen?"

"Um, sure. I can." I glanced at the clock. Six thirty-three. Guests would be arriving soon. Would they walk in on an arrest? Would this whole thing spoil my friend's big day?

I approached Chris with a strained smile. "Hey, Chris. I'm sorry to have to ask you this, but could you help me with something in the kitchen? The caterers are going to be here soon, and I promised I'd have the chafing dishes down out of the cabinet before they arrived, and I'm too short to reach them. Do you mind?"

"I guess not."

He followed along behind me until we got to the kitchen, where Molly and O'Henry were waiting behind closed doors.

"Brewster." O'Henry's opening word let everyone know the seriousness of the moment.

"O'Henry. What are you doing here in uniform?" Chris chuckled. He reached into the upper cabinets and came down with the first chafing dish. "They needed security for this shindig?"

"As a matter of fact, they did."

"Who are you saving them from?" Chris asked with a crooked grin, putting the dish on the counter.

"As a matter of fact," Molly piped up. "You."

Chris paled and backed up till he was leaning against the counter. "What are you talking about?"

"Chris, we need to know your whereabouts on the morning of June eighth," O'Henry said, tapping his foot.

Chris shrugged. "Why? What are you getting at?"

"Just answer his question," Molly said, putting her hand on her hip.

With a smirk, Chris responded, "Well, if you must know, I left my house at eight thirty to stop off at Donut King, like I always do."

"Nothing different about that day. . .at all?" I queried.

"What do you have to do with this, Annie?" he asked. "Are you all in cahoots to frame me for something bogus? 'Cause if you are, you need to know I've got a great Philadelphia attorney, and he's going to—"

"Answer the question, Chris," O'Henry said. "Or wait for your attorney. Whichever one you choose is fine with me. But either way, you're going to need him."

"I've got nothing to hide." Chris shrugged. "I'm sure Kathy will confirm my story. She had a headache that morning and said she didn't feel up to going to church."

Headache, my eye. The only headache she has. . .is you.

"But she was in church that morning." O'Henry gave him a pensive look. "I saw her myself."

"Yes. She surprised me. By the time I got there with the donuts, she was standing on the front steps, chatting with

Sheila. I guess her headache passed."

"Must've been the brisk walk," I threw in. *Sorry, Lord. I couldn't help myself.*

Chris rolled his eyes. "Yes, Kathy has a mind of her own, that's for sure. When she makes up her mind to do something, she does it. I guess she decided to come after all and didn't want to bother me."

"So, you went to the Donut King, as always." Molly crossed her arms and stared him down.

"Sure." Another shrug from Chris let me know he wasn't taking this very seriously.

"Chris. . ." I twisted my hands together, praying for courage to speak my mind. "I happen to know that there were no donuts that morning in the Prime Timers class."

"What?" The creases in his brow deepened. "Of course there were."

"No." I shook my head. "I specifically remember going to lunch with Orin and Sheila that day. When we got to Petracca's, Orin went on and on about how starved he was. How there were *usually* donuts in the classroom, but none that morning. He seemed pretty disappointed."

The tips of Chris's ears turned red.

O'Henry leaned forward, a serious look on his face. "Chris, this is your alibi for that morning? You went to Donut King and then delivered donuts to the classroom, as always?"

"Well, I didn't deliver them myself," Chris said, looking flustered. "I, um, I passed them off to one of the teens and asked him to take them to the classroom."

"Which teen?" Molly asked. "We'll need a full description."

Chris groaned and shook his head. "I don't remember. You expect me to remember which kid I handed them to, when we've got several dozen kids in that youth group? It was some punk teenager with his hair hanging in his eyes. Looked just like all the rest of 'em."

"And you expect me to believe that you—a consummate pro, someone who gets every detail into his front page articles—can't remember who you gave the donuts to?" I asked, drawing close.

Chris's gaze began to dart across the room to the door.

"Oh no you don't." Molly cut him off at the pass. "You're not going anywhere." She reached to put her hand on her side, and I realized for the first time she must be carrying a weapon under that ivory jacket. Very impressive. I certainly wouldn't have to worry about my son's safety.

O'Henry picked up on the look in Chris's eye. "It's time for the truth, Chris. We know for a fact there were no donuts that morning. You might've fooled your wife into thinking you picked them up, but not me. I have over thirty Prime Timers ready to testify there were no donuts."

"So the kid took the donuts and ate them himself. Big deal." Chris's breathing slowed.

"No, Chris." I crossed my arms. "There were no donuts that morning because Donut King was closed down, due to the fire."

Chris paled. "Y–you're crazy."

"No, I'm right," I said. "And you have a lot of explaining to do."

"Kathy has already told us that you left your house at exactly eight forty, just ten minutes before the fire was reported," O'Henry said. "You arrived at the church at five minutes after nine. I saw you come in with my own eyes."

"Y–you're both nuts. And you've got no proof." Funny. I'd never noticed those veins on Chris's forehead before. Looked like he was plenty stressed.

A sound at the door caught my attention. I turned to see Opal standing there in a beautiful blue dress. If we hadn't been in the middle of an arrest, I might've paused to compliment her.

"Kathy took me shopping!" she squealed. "What do you think of my wedding dress? Pretty, huh?" She took one look at Chris, and her vision narrowed. She took a few steps in his direction and put a finger in his face. "You need to be horse-whipped, young man. Writing that mean-spirited article about me was about as low as a person can go."

"Opal, step back," O'Henry said.

"You'll do anything for a headline, won't you?" Opal said, taking a small step backward but never losing her focus on Chris. "Even going so far as to create news when there is none."

Chris's demeanor changed. He pointed at Opal and began to rant. "This crazy old woman is a menace," he spewed. "She needs to be stopped."

Okay. Now we're headed somewhere. Just how far would you go to stop her, Brewster?

He turned to face Opal, drawing so near to her it scared me. "You claim to be a matchmaker, but you don't know the first thing about what you're doing," he continued, the intensity of his voice rising. Now he turned to face the rest of us. "Would you like to hear all the things she told me about my wife before she connected us as a so-called *perfect match?*" He went off on a tangent, a wild look in his eyes, spewing venom all over the place—about Opal and about his wife.

As he continued to rant, I noticed O'Henry quietly unclipping his handcuffs from his belt. Yep. Looked like we were going to have an arrest. . .right here in the kitchen of Clarksborough Community Church, just fifteen minutes before Louise McGillicuddy's wedding. And nothing—or no one—could stop it from going down.

CHAPTER TWENTY-SIX

MATCHLESS LOVE

O'Henry had just slapped the handcuffs on Chris Brewster's wrists when Janetta, Richard, and Elio burst through the door into the kitchen, trays in hand. The pungent smell of Greek food filled the air. As they came through one way, Opal slipped out the other. I didn't blame her. I was tempted to turn and run myself. Instead, I turned to face Janetta, unsure of what to say or do.

Fortunately—or unfortunately—I never had a chance to speak a word.

"Oh Annie!" Janetta wailed. "I was afraid I wouldn't make it! My car had a flat tire, and when Elio came to rescue us, he got Nick's truck stuck in the ditch outside my house. You know how bad the roads are out there, right?"

"Yes, but. . ."

"Oh, I knew you would be upset, and I don't blame you, but Richard and I can still pull this off, I promise. Louise won't know a thing. It's going to be great, just watch and see. We'll get everything set up while the ceremony is going on." She started to tell me about how great the food was going to be, but I couldn't keep up with her. I just kept waiting for O'Henry to say or do something.

"Well, I. . ." I nodded my head toward Chris Brewster, trying to give her a hint, but she kept going.

"The cake is in the car. It turned out great, but I almost lost the top layer when the tire blew. It's a miracle it hung on."

"Janetta," I said, "we need you to—"

I never got to finish. She set a tray on the counter and kept on talking. "We're gonna need some help getting things unloaded from my car. I've got the appetizers and the punch bowl and all sorts of things like napkins and decorative items. Can you guys give us some help?" She gave O'Henry and Chris a pleading look. For a moment. Then, just as quickly, her face paled. "For heaven's sake. You're. . ." She stared at the handcuffs on Brewster's wrists and the scowl on his face then slowly backed out of the room, dragging Richard and Elio with her.

"I love America!" Elio said as the door slammed behind them. "It's just like television!"

"In this show, the bad guy definitely goes to jail," O'Henry muttered, holding a firm grip on our suspect. He proceeded to read Chris his rights, followed by a stern warning. "Now, here's how this is going to go down. We're going to walk through that fellowship hall like nothing's happening. You've already ruined one marriage; you're not going to ruin a perfectly good wedding. Do you understand?"

Chris sucked in a breath and nodded. I wanted to ask him how he'd turn this episode into a headline, if given the opportunity, but didn't. No, we probably wouldn't be seeing any more headlines from Chris Brewster for, say, ten to twenty years.

"Deputy O'Shea is going to walk on one side of you," O'Henry continued, "and I'm going to walk on the other. No one is going to say a word. We're going to walk in a straight line through the crowd until we get to the door. You're not going to pull anything. I hope I make myself plain."

Another nod from Chris. I glanced up at the clock. Ten till seven? Louise must be having fits in the bride's room. I had to get in there to check on her. But, first things first.

I walked to the door leading to the fellowship hall and eased it open, peeking outside. "I see a few folks on the far side of the room," I whispered to O'Henry, "but not many. Likely most everyone is in the sanctuary already."

In a flash, and without anyone being the wiser, the officers ushered Chris through the room. As I opened the door leading to the parking lot, I came face-to-face with Opal and Kathy. Kathy took one look at her husband in handcuffs and melted. She extended her hand in his direction, but O'Henry gave her a stern warning to keep her distance. The tears in her eyes broke my heart, but there was little I could do about them now. No, right now there was really only one thing I needed to do. . .get Louise McGillicuddy down the aisle.

As soon as I watched O'Henry press Brewster into the backseat of his patrol car, I grabbed Opal's hand and said, "Come with me." We raced through the fellowship hall and down the hall, passing the groom-to-be and his brother standing next to Pastor Miller. A quick glance in the sanctuary let me know that we had a packed house. Now, if only I could actually pull this thing off.

Seconds later, we arrived at the bride's room. Before she would let me enter, Opal turned to me with a motherly look on her face.

"Deep breath, Annie. This is her wedding day. She can't know."

"But how are we going to keep it from her?"

"Easy. We play it cool. That's what Sherlock Holmes and Watson would've done, right?"

"Right." I gave her a wink, drew in a calming breath, then knocked on the door. "How's our bride-to-be?" I asked in my most cheerful voice.

Louise turned, and I gasped as I saw her in all her glory. With her hair done and the veil in place, she looked every bit the radiant bride. "Annie. . ." She extended her hand. "I'm glad you're here. I think Teresa's almost got me ready."

"Thanks for your help." I nodded in Teresa's direction. Then, turning back to the lovely bride, I gave her an update. "The caterers are here. The fellowship hall looks great. The groom and best man are perched and ready, and we have a full house. Any questions?"

"Yes, just one." A tear rolled down her cheek. "Is this really happening to me, Annie? Really, truly?"

I wanted to give her a huge hug but didn't dare for fear I'd mess up the dress, hair, or makeup. Instead, I wiped a tear of my own away and nodded. "Oh honey. Yes. It's really, truly happening. There are happily ever afters, and you're living one." Turning to Teresa, I whispered, "And you're going to, too. I can feel it in my gut. Before long, you two will be sisters!"

Opal stood behind me, sniffling. We all turned her direction. Louise took a step toward her and extended a hand. "Opal." The two women stood and stared at each

238 THE PERFECT MATCH

other in silence a moment. "I owe you so much," Louise whispered. "You introduced me to my perfect match. None of this would have happened if not for you."

"Oh sweetie. . ." Opal dabbed her eyes as she spoke. "It wasn't me. It's the Lord. None of this would have happened if not for *Him*."

My heart swelled with joy at those precious words. Looked like Opal had truly made her peace with God.

"I do believe you're right," Louise said with a wink.

Glancing at the clock, I realized the time had come. "It's seven o'clock, Louise." I gestured toward the door. "Are you ready to become Mrs. Nikolas Petracca?"

"Am I ever!" She practically sprinted toward the door, a glorious smile on her face. As she passed by me, she grabbed my hand and whispered, "Oh, by the way, Annie. I don't need you to watch Ruby for me. Teresa has agreed to do it."

A wave of relief passed over me. I'd totally forgotten that she'd asked me to watch her dog!

She and Teresa entered the hallway; then Opal drew near. As she did, I reached to take her into my arms, planting a tender kiss on her soft, wrinkled cheek.

"How do you do it, Annie?" Opal asked, gazing into my eyes. "How in the world do you always figure out who committed the crime?"

"Elementary, my dear Watson," I whispered. "I never take on a case without seeking assistance"—I pointed up— "from the greatest case-solver of all."

CHAPTER ▌▐▐▐ TWENTY-SEVEN

C'MON BABY, LIGHT MY FIRE

About a week after the wedding, Molly asked us to meet with her at Petracca's, claiming she had something important to share. "Bring Opal," she insisted. "This involves her."

We arrived at six o'clock. Elio and Teresa offered us the small party room in the back so we'd have some privacy.

"Molly, what's up?" I asked.

She stood at the head of the table, drawing in a couple of measured breaths. "Okay, I've held on to this information for too long. It's been killing me. I've got to get it off my chest."

Devin gave her a supportive look—my first sign that he actually knew what she was about to say.

"My mother passed away two years ago from cancer," she said. "It was the worst year of my life. I've never known that kind of pain. My dad was long gone. Hadn't seen him since I was fourteen. But I knew I had family in Clarksborough, so I came here looking."

"Family?" I was amazed. "Who? Someone here in town?"

"Yes." Her gaze shifted to the opposite side of the table. "My mom told me the story years ago, but I really didn't have the courage to come to Clarksborough till after she died."

"So. . .who?" Warren asked. "Someone we know?"

Molly nodded slowly, a smile creeping across her face. "Someone you know really well. Someone at this table, in fact."

"What?" We all looked around, our gaze finally landing on the only possible choice.

"Me?" Opal paled. "I. . .I don't understand. How is that possible?"

"Your daughter, Katy. . ."

Molly had no sooner spoken the words than Opal began to cry. "What about Katy?"

Molly's next few words were rushed yet filled with excitement. "She was my grandmother."

"What?" We all spoke the word in unison.

"But that's impossible," Opal said. "Katy never had a child."

Molly nodded, her eyes filled with tears. "She did. She had my mother in the late sixties and gave her up for adoption. She was living in San Francisco at the time. Does that sound familiar?"

Opal nodded. "She was such a wild little thing. Went off to California with all those hippies. I tried to call her dozens of times, but she was so caught up in drugs back then. I couldn't reach her. Her father and I tried. . . ." Opal's tears rushed in little rivers down her cheeks. "Oh, how we tried." She paused to dry her eyes. "Charlie loved that girl so much. And when we got the news that she'd died of a drug overdose, well, he was never the same. He. . .he died of a heart attack just a couple years later."

"I'm so sorry, Grandma!"

At the word *grandma*, Opal began to wail. She couldn't

seem to control her emotions any longer. In that moment, a thousand thoughts went through my mind. *God, you did it! You've not only brought Opal into the body of Christ, You've given her a family of her own!*

Right away, I was reminded of that scripture—oh, where was it?—about how God would make a home for the homeless and would be a father to the orphans and a champion of widows. In one move, He'd done all of those things for Opal and for Molly.

Molly rose and rushed to Opal's side. They held each other and wept. In fact, we all wept. There wasn't a dry eye in the place.

Finally Opal pulled back and looked into Molly's face. "I should've known. That beautiful red hair. Kate was a redhead."

"Was she?" Molly's face lit up with a smile. "I've always wondered where it came from."

"Oh yes. She had glorious red hair, just like her father. And freckles, just like you. I've got pictures galore. But I never dreamed. . ." Opal gazed at Molly with great tenderness. "Oh honey, forgive me. I'm still in shock. Nothing is making sense right now. But I have to know. . .how did you find me?"

"My mom did a lot of legwork," Molly said. "Wrote a lot of letters. She was adopted into a great family, said she always felt loved, but she longed to know about her real family."

Opal shook her head. "It breaks my heart to know Katy had a child and I never got to meet her."

"She wanted to connect with her birth family," Molly said, "but never had the courage. Then, right before she died, she made me promise that I would come. I think she didn't want to leave me without this link to my past."

"I–I'm your link." Opal smiled through her tears.

"Yes, but I still had to go through several channels to find you. In fact. . ." Molly grinned. "I even joined half a dozen online dating services using my middle name and my mom's adopted last name before I figured out that your service wasn't on the Internet."

Well, that explains that!

"Never could figure out much about how to set up a Web page for my services," Opal explained. "And I always liked the personal touch anyway."

"Right." Molly nodded. "I just want you to know that I really tried to reach you. And I tried to tell you who I was— who I *am*—that first week when I came to town. I stopped by your place the same Sunday morning of the fire. But I couldn't make myself knock on the door. I wanted to. . ." A catch in her throat caused the words to stick. "But I couldn't."

Well, so much for the pictures of Molly on the morning of the fire. O'Henry must've known all this. Surely he would have suspected her otherwise.

Opal's smile lit up her face. "Oh honey, I wish you'd come in." After a pause, she added, "On the other hand, I'm glad you weren't there when the fire started. That would've been awful."

"But that's just it. I feel terrible that I wasn't there to protect you." Molly sighed. "But I guess that's all in the past now."

"Looks like a lot of things are in the past," I said.

"I'm just so happy, I could cry." Molly's eyes pooled again. "You have no idea the hours and hours of prayer I've put into this. And who would've guessed I'd end up finding you. . .and a new job." She turned and gave Devin a shy glance. "And so much more."

He beamed, and I thought I saw a hint of tears in his eyes as well.

"God is very good," Molly whispered.

"Yes, He is." Devin echoed. He reached for her hand and gave it a squeeze.

Any questions I might've had about Molly faded with her last comment. Looked like I wouldn't need to have a little chat with Devin about her spiritual state after all.

Opal shook her head and laughed. "Well, go figure. And the Almighty even included me in the deal. I'm a part of something now. I have a family."

"You do." Molly gave her a wink. "If you'll have me."

"Oh you beautiful girl, of course I'll have you!" Opal gave her at least twenty kisses on her freckled cheeks.

As Opal released her hold, Devin pulled Molly into his arms and gave her a little kiss on the forehead. She stared at him with the sweetest smile I've ever seen. Opal looked on with an "I told you so" look on her face then turned my way, gazing at me with such tenderness in her expression that I almost burst into tears right then and there. I reached to give her a hug then whispered the perfect words, burning a path straight from my heart. . .

"This is what it feels like to have a family, Opal."

She clutched my hand and whispered through her tears, "At last."

CHAPTER ⛫ TWENTY-EIGHT

THE PERFECT MATCH

Exactly two months to the day after Louise and Nick tied the knot, the whole town of Clarksborough gathered together to help Opal with the rebuilding of her property.

"Do you think you'll go on with the matchmaking service?" Devin asked.

"Oh my, no!" Opal proclaimed. "I'm about to celebrate my eighty-fourth birthday. No point in working at my age. Besides, I've got family to care for now." She reached over to give Molly a hug. "We need a home big enough to accommodate us. Well, until Molly gets married someday." Opal's thinly plucked eyebrows elevated as she looked Devin's way. For a moment, a look of panic registered in his eyes. Oblivious, Opal kept talking. "And even then, I'll want to have enough space for all the babies. Oh, I have so much to look forward to!"

Molly blushed at that announcement. "One thing at a time, Gran-Gran!"

Opal took a few steps in my direction. "Annie, I just wanted you to know something."

"What?"

"There was a time I thought I wouldn't find a place to

fit in. Thanks to you, I really feel like I'm part of something now. Something bigger than myself, I mean. I've found my great-granddaughter, and I've got a host of friends at that church of yours."

"Yes, but you need to start calling it *your* church," I admonished her. "You've been a member for almost two months now, remember?"

"Right, right." She nodded. "And I've met a lot of folks. Mighty nice folks." She gave me a wink. I knew for a fact she'd had her eye on one person in particular—seventy-nine-year-old Roger Kratz. Never mind that he was five years younger. That didn't seem to bother her one bit.

Yes, things had certainly come full circle. No doubt about that. Opal Lovelace was our church's newest darling. And she'd made good on her promise to bless the Sonnier family financially. Of course, she could really afford to do that, now that the insurance company had decided to pay to rebuild her home.

On top of all of this, Richard and Janetta had stunned us all with their announcement. They were getting married in two months, and guess who they wanted to coordinate their wedding? Yours truly. Could I really pull it off in such a short time? Not unless the Lord worked a miracle.

Of course, He did happen to be in the miracle-working business.

Off in the distance, I watched as someone now very near and dear to my heart approached.

"Annie." Kathy Brewster extended her hand to grab mine. "How are you doing?"

"I think the more appropriate question would be, 'How are *you* doing?' "

Her eyes filled with tears, and she nodded. "Well, I'll tell you. . .this whole thing caught me totally off guard. I knew Chris would do just about anything for a headline, but I never figured. . ." She shook her head, a tear now rolling down her cheek.

"None of us did." I reached to hug her. "But nobody blames you, Kathy. You couldn't have known."

"I know, but when I think of poor Opal, all she's lost. . ." Kathy nodded in Opal's direction. "It breaks my heart."

"She's pretty resilient, especially now that she's found Molly. But. . .will you stay on in Clarksborough while Chris is. . ." I didn't want to say the words.

"In prison?" Kathy nodded. "I'll stay here. I'm going to try to keep the paper going, actually. I've never told anyone this before, but I've always been a writer."

"No kidding?"

"Oh yes. In fact, several of the shows I've directed or starred in were my own."

"I had no idea."

"I know now that God gave me this ability so that I could somehow salvage the paper. It's my chance to make things up to the community and a way to make a living. And I know that Chris will be happy to see it continue." She drew in a breath. "Annie, I realize that Chris did something awful. Terrible. I feel sick every time I think of what could've happened to Opal. But I can't help but think that God finally has him in a place where he might just listen."

"Listen?"

"To the voice of the Holy Spirit." Kathy squeezed my hand. "Janetta has been telling me so many great things about the church's prison ministry. Just look at the turnaround in Richard's life. You know? Maybe these next few years Chris will experience the same."

"And you're willing to wait and see?"

"For now, anyway." She shrugged and gave me a woeful look. "With everything that's just happened, I don't think this is the time to make a fast decision. And besides, Chris really needs me right now. He's never needed me before." After a pause, she added, "Does that make sense?"

"Yes. I'm not sure what I'd do in your situation, but I do think it's admirable that you're willing to give your marriage a chance."

"It's not the marriage I'm giving a chance," she whispered. "It's God. I'm giving *Him* a chance to do a work in my husband's life, even if it means we're never together as a couple again."

Wow.

"So, I plan to stay really busy with the paper," Kathy explained. "That will keep my mind off things." After a quick smile, she looked around at the crowd. "Where are Opal and Molly? I need to talk to them. I understand they have a story that tops any headline Chris ever came up with. I just want to get their permission to run it."

"Oh, they'll be thrilled! Molly and Opal are quite a team. You're going to have a blast talking to them. And"—I leaned in close—"while you're at it, you might as well know that any of Opal's stories need to be double-checked. She's in the beginning stages of Alzheimer's."

"What? How long have you known?"

"We'd noticed some suspicious activities all along—missing items, putting things in the wrong place, getting lost or discombobulated, short-term memory loss. Those sorts of things. Molly finally talked her into going to the doctor a couple of weeks ago, and he confirmed what I already thought I knew. She's on a medication that's supposed to slow down the progression of the disease, but just know that her stories are sometimes a bit. . ."

"Off?"

"Yes." I nodded. "For example, that whole story about the fire in her bedroom? She blamed it on the dog, but Warren and I have definitely come to the conclusion—at least in our own minds—that she knocked that candle over herself. Alzheimer's is a tricky disease, so you can't really blame the person who doesn't remember. You just have to move on and face one challenge at a time."

"True."

"If you have any questions for your article, I can answer them. Or Molly can. She and Opal are joined at the hip these days."

At that moment, Molly came rushing my way. "Annie, you need to come. Devin wants to get a picture of all of us in front of Gran-Gran's place before the first beam goes up. You ready?"

"Am I ready to start rebuilding? To help someone I love put her life back together again? You bet!"

I looked at the throng of people in front of the property, tears filling my eyes as I watched Maddy scramble into her mommy's outstretched arms. They would be leaving in the morning for their new home in New York. Every time I thought about it, a lump the size of an orange filled my throat. What would I do without them? Sure, Spike would be just a few blocks away at Candy's house, but he could hardly replace my baby girl!

"You coming?" Molly called out again. "We can't do this without you."

We can't do this without you.

For the first time, I realized what the Lord had done. In so many ways, He'd refined me for the work ahead.

As I pondered the many changes in my life of late, a familiar voice rang out behind me. "Annie Peterson. . . a penny for your thoughts."

I turned to see Warren, the love of my life.

"Oh, I was just thinking about. . ." I laughed. Narrowing the list might be difficult.

"All of Janetta and Richard's wedding plans?" he prompted me.

"No, but I should be! Warren, I have so much to do. They haven't given me much lead time on their wedding. We've got to pick out the invitations, figure out the reception theme, decide on colors for the bridesmaids' dresses. . ."

To my great surprise, Warren put his hand over my mouth.

"Annie." He gazed at me, his eyes twinkling. "Don't you ever stop for a minute?" He shook his head. "No wedding plans. Not right now. And no mysteries. I have something I've been trying to tell you."

He released his hand from my mouth, and I stared into his eyes. *What are you up to, Warren Peterson?*

"I've done something."

"Oh no. You didn't quit your job, did you? Not with the economy in such bad shape. I know you want to retire, but—"

"No, honey. I didn't quit my job. I booked a vacation."

"A vacation?" I stepped back and crossed my arms. "Where are you going?"

"Where are *we* going." He grinned. "*We* are going to Niagara Falls for a second honeymoon, ten weeks from today."

My breath caught in my throat. I'd wanted to go to Niagara Falls for our real honeymoon nearly thirty years ago. Was my dream of seeing the falls up close really coming true?

"You always put everyone else first, Annie," Warren said. "And that's admirable. It's part of what makes you, you." He grinned and kissed my nose. "But this time we're doing something for you. I've scheduled four days at a hotel near the falls, and I've also planned a spa day for you in the middle of it."

A spa day? I could almost see the look of envy on Sheila's face now.

"While we're there, you're not going to solve any cases, make any phone calls—"

"But—" I started to argue. How would I keep up with the kids? Make sure Candy was feeling okay? Check on Maddy?

"You're also not going to eat any diet foods or exercise," Warren said. "This whole thing is about kicking back and relaxing. Having fun."

After pausing to reflect, I smiled. Maybe I could actually

lay down my workload long enough to enjoy some one-on-one time with the man I loved. Silly that I even had to think twice about it.

My heart began to thump out of control as I spoke: "Warren, I have something to tell you."

"What's that?" he asked, tracing my cheek with the tip of his finger.

"I just have to say the words out loud, even though you've known it all along."

"What's that?" He gave me a playful wink.

"Warren Peterson. . ." I giggled a little, hoping I could get the rest to come out without sounding too silly. "Warren Peterson. . .you are my perfect match."

Award-winning author Janice Hanna, who also writes under the name Janice Thompson, has published more than sixty books for the Christian market, crossing genre lines to write cozy mysteries, historicals, romances, nonfiction books, devotionals, children's books, and more. Her passion? Making readers laugh! Janice currently serves as vice president of the Christian Authors Network (christianauthorsnetwork.com) and was named the 2008 Mentor of the Year by the American Christian Fiction Writers organization. She is passionate about her faith and does all she can to share the joy of the Lord with others, which is why she particularly enjoys writing.

Janice lives in Spring, Texas, where she leads a rich life with her family, a host of writing friends, and two mischievous dachshunds. She does her best to keep the Lord at the center of it all. You can find out more about Janice at www.janicehannathompson.com or www.freelancewritingcourses.com.

A Letter to Our Readers

Dear Readers:

In order that we might better contribute to your reading enjoyment, we would appreciate you taking a few minutes to respond to the following questions. When completed, please return to the following: Fiction Editor, Barbour Publishing, Inc., P.O. Box 719, Uhrichsville, OH 44683.

1. Did you enjoy reading *The Perfect Match* by Janice Hanna?
    ❏ Very much. I would like to see more books like this.
    ❏ Moderately—I would have enjoyed it more if _____
    _____
    _____

2. What influenced your decision to purchase this book?
    (Check those that apply.)
    ❏ Cover   ❏ Back cover copy   ❏ Title   ❏ Price
    ❏ Friends   ❏ Publicity   ❏ Other

3. Please check your age range:
    ❏ Under 18   ❏ 18–24   ❏ 25–34
    ❏ 35–45   ❏ 46–55   ❏ Over 55

4. How many hours per week do you read? _____

Name _____

Occupation _____

Address _____

City_____ State_____ Zip_____

E-mail _____

Other
HOMETOWN MYSTERIES
from Barbour Publishing

Nursing a Grudge

 Missing Mabel

Advent of a Mystery

 Nipped in the Bud

May Cooler Heads Prevail